on Myself

I Brought It on Myself

Carrie Thigpen

URBAN BOOKS
http://www.urbanbooks.net

URBAN SOUL is published by

Urban Books
10 Brennan Place
Deer Park, NY 11729

ISBN-13: 978-1-59983-036-0
ISBN-10: 1-59983-036-1

First Printing: November 2007

10 9 8 7 6 5 4 3 2 1

Printed in the United States of America

Dedication

To my children

Jay Alexander Moore
Stacey Denise Moore
Toni Loretta Thigpen

And to the memory of

Wayne Thomas Russell
1958–1996

Chapter 1

Again, nothing was going right. My money: as usual I didn't have any; my man: he didn't know how to act so I finally had to get rid of him; my children: I was always going out of my way to sacrifice for them. Money, men, and children. People can say what they wanna say—these are the three things that can throw a monkey wrench in any woman's life.

I was wondering where I could have possibly gone wrong: why was my life such a mess? After working fourteen days straight, I finally got a night off from the midnight shift at 7-Eleven, and after six hours of sleeping in my bed at night like a normal person, it finally hit me. It hit me hard too, ya'll—*real* hard. The expression "like a ton of bricks" wasn't even a drop in the bucket in describing the hit I'm talking about.

It was about 5:00 on a Sunday morning when I shot straight up in bed and looked straight ahead while in my mind I raced through my childhood home in Cleveland, Ohio . . . 254 N. Vine Avenue, journeying through each part of the house recalling its layout and décor.

There was a tiny foyer (about four by four square feet) between the front door and the door that actually led into the living room. In that space was a dusty little rug that hid a skeleton key garnished with a dirty ribbon, purposefully placed there to allow my sister Liz, who was three years older than me, and I entrance into our home for lunch during the school week.

The living room was very large and filled with old-fashioned furniture and was adjacent to the dining room, which was always dark and served as a catchall for everything from books, bicycles, skates, clothes, papers, tools, to a whole lot of trash and dust. Under all that clutter was the dining-room furniture, which was hardly ever seen until Thanksgiving and Christmas.

The kitchen was of average size and for some reason always seemed too hot. In the corner of the kitchen directly across from the back door were the steps that led down to the basement.

Upstairs in the front of the house was my mom and dad's room, which was without question off limits. Today, most children just walk in their parents' room and help themselves to whatever they want like it's nothing, and most of the time without even asking. I shook my head as I thought of how much things have changed.

There was Liz's room, which held just as strict a "keep out" warning as my parents' room did. Believe it or not, I was more afraid of going in Liz's room than I was my mom and dad's! My brother Jr. occupied the attic whenever he was home, which was rarely, as he served in the navy. Of course, there was a small bathroom, and finally at the end of the hall was the bedroom that I shared with my baby sister, Clarita.

And that's where it all happened.

I was trying to get ready for either school or church—I can't remember clearly which one—but it was definitely one of the two because those were the only two places I ever went. Anyway, my mother had sent me upstairs to find a red blouse. I'd already tried reporting to her two or three times that I couldn't find it, but keep in mind it was the sixties, when mommas weren't doing a whole lot of reasoning or listening to a whole lot of explanations. When she sent me for the blouse that final time, I knew that I had better not come back down without it.

Once more, I searched high and low until I ran out of places to look. Defeated, I sat on my bed and began to cry; I was doomed. As I pulled myself together to go back downstairs and face whatever disastrous consequence awaited me, something red in the springs under the corner of my bed caught my eye. It was the blouse. At first I was happy, but then a line of different emotions quickly began to form, each anxiously pushing its way to the front.

"Happiness" was quickly shoved out of the way by "Relief," telling me that now I didn't have to worry about whatever consequence was waiting for me downstairs had I gone down again without the blouse. Then came the all-famous "Confusion," who wanted to know why hadn't I found the blouse a long time ago; after all, hadn't I searched the room over from top to bottom including the closet and dresser drawers only to now finally find the blouse in plain view? Then I thought about my mother again as "Pride" nudged his way to the front and I imagined her face when I went downstairs again, this time with the blouse. Then it was "Scared's" turn, making me wonder what my momma would do when I told her where I finally found the blouse after all that time. Last but not least was "Anger." Oh yes, that ever-popular Anger, who somehow always manages to force his way into anybody's and everybody's mind in some way or another. Hardly giving "Uncertain" half a chance, somehow Anger always suddenly appears to volunteer his services. He's usually Confusion's biggest threat, and this time, again, Anger won. When Anger came to the front of the line, that's when I started to cuss.

I began to cuss God out—*all the way out*—sparing none of the bad words that I knew. Since I was only five or six, I only knew a few cusswords, but had I known more, I would've used them too because I was just that mad at Him.

The more I thought about it, the more I actually remembered the words I said when I cussed God out. GOD, who predestined my life before I was even born. GOD, who created me in His own image and placed me here on earth for His Glory. GOD, who loved me so much that He chose to die in my place so that I could live eternally. GOD. The all powerful, almighty, all-knowing, ever-loving GOD cussed out by a five-year-old all because she wasn't able able to find her red blouse. Just the thought sent chills all through my body. Yeah, that had to be it. This was definitely where I went wrong.

And now, as I thought about the events of my life that had taken place from that day to this, I began to wonder if I ever would finish paying for that great mistake . . .

Chapter 2

"Ma, can I have breakfast now?" My baby, Terra, stood in the entranceway of my bedroom with wide eyes. I had heard her stirring about but had paid it little attention, being so lost in my thoughts. She rubbed her eyes and squinted at me, reminding me that once again, I would have to replace her glasses. This would make it the third time this year; the first pair had been lost, the second, stepped on and broken. Where was I going to come up with the money to buy yet another pair of frames? One thing for sure, it wasn't up for question; Terra needed them and wouldn't be able to go much longer without them.

Thinking it was still far too early for breakfast, I started to tell her to wait, but as I glanced over at the clock, I realized three hours had passed since my rude awakening. I normally cooked breakfast for Terra on Sunday mornings before church, but today I could hardly pull myself from the bed.

"Yeah, go ahead and make some cereal. Be careful, now. Don't go making no big mess in there like you always do, you hear me?" She was already in the kitchen before I could finish the last sentence. I couldn't help but chuckle to myself; that child sure did love to eat.

It was now just Terra and me, both making our way down life's path with me leading as best I could, which meant working long nights, scraping pennies, and cutting corners to make ends meet. Sometimes those ends did manage to touch each other; other times they were miles apart. My trouble with my money was probably the first manifestation of what felt like a curse that I'd brought on myself. In an instant, I was back to that big old house on Vine Avenue.

I had never been too afraid of taking a risk as long as my very life wasn't jeopardized in the process, so one day I took a chance and went to explore the forbidden territory of my parents' room. It didn't even have to be said, it was just understood that we kids were not allowed in there. And if we were ever given the opportunity to visit my parents' room for any length of time, it was almost like being king or queen for a day. Apparently, this particular day, I was feeling adventurous, knowing that Mom was occupied downstairs with my Aunt Mary, and there was no one else in the house but me.

Stopping all movement, I listened carefully from my room to make sure that Mom and Aunt Mary were deep in conversation. If the stairs didn't creak so badly, I would have tried to sneak down a few to hear them more clearly, but taking the chance of being caught eavesdropping on grown-up conversation was not a risk I was prepared to take that day. Assured by their cackling chatter and outbursts of laughter, I set out on my mission. Just by looking at the distance between my room and theirs, I should have known better; simply walking up the hallway to the door (which remained closed at all times, to confirm the warning to keep out) seemed like the walk of doom. Nonetheless, I made my approach, stopping several times along the way for a sound check. Finally reaching my destination, I slowly opened the door and tiptoed in.

Like a child scouting for presents at Christmastime, I sneaked around the room looking for treasures and riches untold. I tried on several of Mom's church hats while I gave a silent mock testimony in the mirror; took a whiff of all of her perfumes, making sure not to get a single drop on myself; and just basically messed with things that I knew I had no business touching in the first place until I figured out that there was really no big deal about their room at all. The secrecy behind their ever-closed door was far too overrated.

Just as I was coming to the end of my excursion, I struck gold. For no reason in particular, I became curious about what could be on top of this tall, handmade dresser settled against the back wall. Quietly, I lifted a chair from the corner, moved it to the dresser, slowly stood on it, and peered over the dresser's top. In the midst of several miscellaneous items and dusty odds and ends was a small wooden bowl that held about ten silver dollars. My eyes stretched wide, having never seen that much money shining and gleaming in one place before. It took no time at all for me to dig my hand in the bowl, take every coin, and leave the room with my treasures as quickly as I could.

For the next week and a half, I may as well have been the richest woman in the world. I took the long way to school, stopping by the store to fill my book bag with candy, gum, and cheap toys, but pretty soon, the money was gone and long forgotten.

It was a couple of weeks later when my dad noticed the missing money. Instead of questioning both Liz and me, he automatically accused Liz. Liz swore she knew nothing about the money, but Daddy beat her unmercifully, certain that she had taken it. Ridden with guilt, I hid in my room trying to block out her cries, and praying that her beating would come to a quick end . . . but it didn't. I privately cried with her, not from physical pain, though, but from a new kind of pain—the pain from my conscience. It was only about a week later when I mistakenly told on myself.

Daddy had been working on a little footstool on the back porch and needed to even up its legs before joining the parts together. Humming a tune to himself, he rose from the back steps, did a quick search in the dining room and kitchen drawers, then called out, "Anybody seen my handsaw?"

With absolutely no thought, I blurted out, "Yes, sir! It's on the top of your dresser." I said it with a big smile, proud that I'd been able to resolve his dilemma, but never even realizing the trouble that I had just gotten myself into. My father went upstairs to get the saw, not catching on to what had just happened. Unfortunately for me, my mother was a little sharper than my dad. She said nothing right then, but instead waited until the next day, catching me off guard.

"How did you know your daddy's saw was on top

of the dresser, Ivy?" she posed nonchalantly. Instantly, panic struck and every word I ever knew left my mind. I had absolutely nothing to say; I'd been caught. Instead of answering, I just began to cry. "You took that money, didn't you Ivy?" I never answered. I didn't have to.

Now I didn't have the "wait-till-your-father-gets-home" type of mother; on the contrary, Arnetta Freeman certainly needed no help with keeping Liz and me in line, issuing discipline whenever (and wherever) it was needed. But this particular time was different; when she made no moves to punish me, I knew what was to come. Voluntarily, I went to my room to await the punishment that I knew I would get when my father came home. In my mind, it was like sitting on death row.

Six o'clock came much too fast that day, but still not fast enough as far as Momma was concerned. Daddy couldn't have had more than one foot across the threshold when I heard Momma start in on him. She didn't even say "Hi" first.

"Miss Ivy got the money, and Miss Liz got the beating."

"What you say?" Daddy asked, having not heard her. Momma was too glad to repeat it, not only because she was telling on me, but also because she was too happy to rub his false accusation in his face. Like other married couples, I suppose, Momma and Daddy used to argue a lot, and just like every other woman, Momma loved it when she was right and Daddy was wrong.

In a matter of seconds, Daddy was upstairs. I had counted the steps hundreds of times and knew that there were definitely thirteen, but I only heard him take about five or six steps. His belt was already in his hand by the time he got to my room, and he wasn't there to talk first. That beating had to be the most horrible beating that I had experienced in my life.

Although it's been many years since that time, I can still hear the cries of my sister Liz as she took a terrible beating for the money I stole. And to this day, my money ain't been right since.

Chapter 3

The sound of the ringing phone snapped me out of my semitrance-like state back to reality. Glancing at the Caller ID first, I lifted the receiver to my face.

"Hey, girl," I said with no enthusiasm.

"How'd you sleep? You feeling all right? You going to church today?" Gloria pushed out in one big breath.

"I need to go, but I don't know." My eyes quickly glanced around the room at the ton of boxes that had to be emptied, clothes that needed to be hung, and straightening that needed to be done. "I need to try to get this house together."

"Well, that's why I was seeing if you were going to go to church, 'cause if you want me to, I can come over and help you unpack and get settled," she offered. "Girl, I know you gotta be tired."

Right away, I took Gloria up on her offer. God would understand if I sat at home one Sunday, I reasoned. And it wasn't like I would just be lying around on the couch and reading a magazine. I really did need to get settled into my new place.

"How soon you coming?" I asked, making a weak effort to swing my legs over the side of my box spring and mattress, which were piled together on the floor since my bed hadn't been put up yet.

"I can be on my way in about twenty minutes. Y'all ate yet?"

"Terra had some cereal a little while ago, but you know how she is. If you bring something, she's not going to hurt your feelings by turning it down." I chuckled.

"Well, I'ma stop and get some biscuits or something from McDonald's before they stop serving breakfast. We can have the house put together by this evening."

"Thanks, Gloria." I smiled. "I'll see you in a little bit."

Gloria had to be the best in the world. We had been through so much together in our adult years, having each other's back through thick and thin.

Coincidentally, as I lifted myself from my mattress and padded my way to the bathroom, I knocked over an old photo album that had been sitting on top of a box right outside my bedroom door. It smacked against the floor, causing a stiff, hard Polaroid to protrude from its side. It was a picture of me, Gracie Wallace, and Tawanna Monk. At one time in my young life, we too had been best friends; Tawanna was my best friend at school, and Gracie was my best church friend. I couldn't recall how it had happened that the three of us were all together for this one particular shot, but just seeing the two of them together in one photo brought a smile to my face because of how much they differed. Everything from their appearance, their personality, and even their home life was totally opposite.

Gracie was short and thick; Tawanna was tall and thin. Gracie had very dark, ashy skin that most of the time smelled like pee; Tawanna had a smooth, medium brown complexion that smelled like Jergen's lotion, Ivory soap, or a combination of the two. Gracie's hair was short and nappy; Tawanna had coal black hair that was always permed (that's right, *permed*—the girl was getting perms in the sixties!) and styled in long curls that bounced on her shoulders whenever she moved. Gracie's house was cluttered with clothes, toys, animals (real and fake), and people all the time. Her room, which she shared with her two sisters, stayed junky and, just like Gracie, always smelled like pee. Tawanna's house was spotless, filled with beautiful furniture, and smelled like pine, and she was hardly ever allowed to have company in her bedroom, which she shared with no one.

Gracie had a very sweet personality. She was very quiet and soft-spoken, and eager to share anything and everything from material things to emotions. When anyone was happy, Gracie was also happy for that person. When anyone was sad, Gracie was too, even though nine times out of ten the person's trouble had nothing to do with her, for Gracie rarely did anything to get in trouble. Tawanna, on the other hand, made little of other people's good fortunes and found their misfortunes funny. She was overall a very mean person who felt she had to call the shots, and anyone was lucky if she chose him or her to be her friend.

The thing that made me laugh the most about

their differences, though, was this: Not only was Tawanna a lousy fighter, but she only had a younger brother so she had no one to help her fight if needed. So when somebody intimidated or threatened Tawanna, she would run home crying to tell her momma and stayed in the house until things cooled off. If anybody messed with Gracie, on the other hand, she had two real sisters, a foster sister, a real brother, a foster brother, and a vicious family dog. However, she didn't need any of them for help; Gracie could fight like a man. I wasn't much of a fighter myself and wished Gracie had been around just a few short months ago when I could have used someone who knew how to land a solid punch or two.

Gloria arrived with a large bag holding three big breakfast platters and another bag swung from her arm holding a gallon jug of orange juice and a package of Styrofoam cups.

"I guess we are going to have to eat on the floor for now, or otherwise on our laps," I said, heaving a pile of blankets from the couch, trying to make room for us to sit. Terra had been nestled in one corner of the couch watching cartoons all morning; other than her little spot, there had been no other sitting room. I tossed the blankets in the middle of the floor and shooed Terra off the couch, making her think she'd be more comfortable sprawled out on the blankets. Just like I anticipated, she dove for the covers and landed on her belly in laughter. "Sit here, Gloria." I motioned with one hand, but she walked over to the kitchen looking for any free spot where she could pour the juice. "Since we aren't going to church today, the least I can do is watch it on TV while I eat."

"Yeah, you right about that. I need to get some word in to get my week started off right," Gloria answered over her shoulder. "Did you get your cable hooked up already? Turn on Creflo."

"Do we gotta watch him?" I whined, scanning the room for the remote. "His church too big and modernized; I wanna watch some old-time church." My nostalgia had taken over, making me long for the hand-clapping, foot-stomping church atmosphere I'd grown up in. I flipped through channels, passing right by Changing Your World, Potter's House, Breakthrough, and Lakewood while Gloria screamed for me to stop each time. Maybe Bishop G. E. Patterson could give me what I was looking for. Before I could find him, Gloria snatched the remote out of my hand and began channel surfing herself.

"By the time you find something, church will be over, and folks will be done went back to sinning until next Sunday." We laughed as she flipped back to Bishop Jakes, then settled in on the couch and began eating.

As much as I like Jakes, he just couldn't hold my attention this particular Sunday. My eyes were fixed on the TV screen while I forked eggs in my mouth, but my mind was far away in Cleveland.

Chapter 4

Every Sunday, Momma, Liz, myself, and Clarita would go to church and stay all day. I don't mean the kind of all day that only equates to four or five hours; I mean *all* day . . . morning to night. Daddy hardly ever came and probably enjoyed the time that we were away not causing some kind of ruckus and commotion in the house, and we really didn't mind that much, though, either. First of all, we went to a fairly large church where something was always going on, and secondly, we didn't want to miss out on anything that might have happened had we not been there.

Momma would start cooking at the crack of dawn every Sunday morning to make sure everything was ready by the time we had to leave for church. I can still remember smelling the fried chicken cooking on the stove top and cake baking in the oven. These were familiar breakfast scents, although breakfast was normally eggs, grits, toast, and general breakfast foods. She would feed us as soon as we woke up, trying to keep us out of her way while she turned chicken and stirred vegetables. It would smell so good that we'd beg for a little sample of what she was cooking for dinner as well. Sometimes she gave in and gave us a chicken drumstick and a small piece of cake, but most of the time all we got was a warning of what we *would* get a taste of if we didn't leave her alone, go upstairs, and start getting dressed.

Of course, we went upstairs and messed around before we actually started getting ready. Sometimes we played, but most of the time Liz and I fought, with Liz often winning. I'm not sure how we did it, but regardless of how long we played or fought, we still managed to get ready before our mom got upstairs. It's almost like we had an internal alarm clock to warn us that our "mess around" time was up, but it never failed. By the time we heard our mom coming up those steps, we were putting on and buckling that last patent leather Sunday shoe.

Then it would get very busy, because it was time to help our mom get ready. For some reason, she would often get ready for church in my and Clarita's room.

"Ivy, go get my white blouse—the one with the ruffles hanging in my closet. Liz, get my black shoes—the shiny ones, now."

"Ma, I can't find it!" I was always the one who couldn't find something.

"You *better* find it!" Momma yelled back.

"Here, Ma." Somehow Liz always found what Mom sent her after. She really made me sick.

"Not them, the other ones." I looked at Liz and smirked. This was after I made sure that she wasn't looking back at me, of course.

"I didn't see any other ones."

"Where you get them from?"

"In your closet."

"Look under my bed, then."

"Here, Ma." I was so glad to have finally found her blouse, only to have my feelings crushed again.

"Not that one, Ivy. I said the one with ruffles."

"That *is* the one with ruffles."

"That's *not* ruffles, Ivy! That's lace! Don't you know the difference between ruffles and lace?"

"Ma!" Liz yelled from my parents' room down the hall.

"What?"

"I don't see any shoes under your bed either!"

"Well, where in the world could they be? Oh, I know! Look downstairs beside the chair I always sit in. And while you down there, turn off the oven."

"Here, Ma." I had finally found the right one.

"Thanks. Now go look in my top drawer and get me a pair of stockings. They're right in the front corner of the top drawer, Ivy. Hurry up, now."

"Okay."

"Liz!"

"Yes?"

"You taking too long down there. What you doing? You *better* not be digging in that food!" Momma knew us too well.

"Huh?"

"You heard me!"

"I'm coming!"

"Lord have mercy! I just put a run in my new stockings! Oh well, I don't have time to change now. Come on Liz and Ivy and help me put my girdle on." In the midst of our pulling and tugging, the phone rang. "Get the phone, Liz. If it's Mary, tell her we'll be ready by the time she gets here. Come on Ivy, *pull!*" I tugged at the girdle as hard as I could. I don't think my mom realized how hard of a task that was for a little girl of no more than eight or nine years old. That was too much work for me. We would pull and tug so much that one time Liz and I actually lifted Momma off the floor.

"When I grow up, I'm not wearing no girdle. I'm going to let my butt shake all it want to," I stated. Momma cracked up.

"Liz, was that Mary?"

"Yes. She said she's on her way."

"I thought so, and I still have to finish putting my clothes on. Come on Liz and Ivy, *please* hurry up! Ivy, why your shoes look like that?" she asked, taking note of my overly shiny shoes.

"She put grease on them to make them real shiny. I told her not to do it!"

"No I didn't! Shut up!"

"You did so, and don't tell me to shut up, because shut don't go up, prices do. Take my ad—"

"The both of you better shut up! This is not the time to be fussing with Mary on the way and we're not even ready yet. We're *never* ready! It don't make sense! Go downstairs and get everything together— I'm coming. And I *better* not hear no fussing down there either, you hear me?"

"Yes."

Of course the fussing never stopped; we just kept it at a lower volume. By "everything," Momma meant our coats, her coat, her Bible, her Sunday school book, her pocketbook, her "flats" (shoes), her freshly ironed choir robe, and the picnic basket.

I'll never forget that picnic basket. It wasn't really a basket, but a red insulated food bag that our mom stuffed so full every Sunday that the zipper finally broke. It was amazing how much food that bag could hold. We had to be extra careful of how we carried it so that nothing would fall out of it because of the broken zipper. I often wondered why we never just got a new bag. I think our mom thought that as long as we were careful enough when we carried it, she wouldn't have to buy another one and, as she did about a lot of things, Momma thought right.

While we waited for Momma to come downstairs and our Aunt Mary to come, the arguing started all over again. It usually started over who looked the best, and because this was in the sixties, when skin complexion was a big deal and Liz's was lighter than mine, this was the first thing she always started out with.

"At least I ain't black like you," she would say.

"I don't care. At least my hair is longer and my face is not bumpy like yours" was my defense.

"I know you don't care, because care don't get you nowhere! And Momma told you not to wear your shoes like that no more either." I liked to wear the straps of my baby doll shoes behind my heels instead of on top of my foot like they were supposed to be, because it looked more grown up.

"You just trying to copy off me. I'm telling. Ma! "

"Shut up down there!" By the time Mom heard Liz calling her, I had switched the straps like they were supposed to be. When I heard Momma's reply, I looked at Liz with a victorious smile as I switched them back like I had them.

"Blackie."

"Bald head."

"Tar baby."

"Bumpy face."

"That's why Johnny broke up with you and go with me now, because you too black."

"I don't care. I don't want that big-eared boy no more anyway. I go with Mitchell Nathane. He asked me last Sunday. I'm telling him yes today." Liz's mood instantly changed.

"For real?" she asked, with stretched eyes. Every girl in the church would have loved to go with Mitchell Nathane, because he was so cute. He had pretty brown skin and naturally wavy hair—two definite pluses for a colored boy during the sixties.

"Yep. He gave me a ring and everything." A smile came on my face as I thought about the Cracker Jack ring Mitchell gave me on the previous Sunday.

"You lying. Let me see it."

"It's broke now." The smile changed into a frown as I remembered how quickly and easily the ring had just broken in half.

"Because you lying. Why didn't you show it to me *before* it broke?"

"Because I . . ."

"Because you lying. That's all you do is lie, with your black self."

"I am not lying, because when . . ."

Beep-beeeeep!

"Ma! Aunt Mary's here!"

"Okay! Go ahead and start taking the stuff out. I'm coming!"

Although the ride to church was only about fifteen minutes or so, it seemed like much longer, because Aunt Mary didn't let us fuss, play, or even talk barely above a whisper in her car. She couldn't stand sassy children and didn't mind slapping anybody's child who got that way in her presence. In that day parents didn't mind other adults correcting their children when they got out of line. I couldn't help but think that this was a good thing, because children were much more respectful back then than they are today. Only thing was that the one correction from the "other adult" was never enough, regardless of what the correction was. After his or her correction, the other adult would take you by your hand to your Momma, tell her what happened, and it didn't matter what the other adult said, he or she was right. Then your Momma would get you again!

Aunt Mary had some kind of bone disorder that made her fingers bend forward at each of the joints, so her hands couldn't open all the way. Her hands were real hard too, so when Aunt Mary slapped you, it wasn't a real slap, but rather a punch. Once, we were on the way to church, and Aunt Mary was talking to Mom about a lady who went to another church named Sister Broadway. About that time this particular song was popular and I blurted it out before I realized the consequence.

"You talking about Sister Funky Broadway?" I looked over at Liz expecting her to laugh, but Liz knew better.

The next thing I knew, I saw Aunt Mary's deformed hand coming toward my leg and I felt like I was just hit by a two by four. As far as I could remember, that was my very first bruise. My mom never said a word. Don't misunderstand; Aunt Mary was my father's sister. That meant besides being my mother's sister-in-law, she was also my mom's very best friend, and she loved Liz and me to no end. She just didn't like sassy children, so when we were sassy, Aunt Mary would have no problem voicing (or showing) her disapproval.

Chapter 5

Church started with Sunday school, where everyone would be put into separate classes according to age. Then there was morning service. Although long, it was never boring. It began with the choir marching in. As far back as I can remember, the choir always marched in by the very same song. Everyone in the church stood, and the choir came in with perfect harmony:

"Ho-ly, Ho-ly, Hooo-Leee!
Lord God Almiii-ghty!
Early in the morrrr-ning,
The sun shall riiise to Theee!"

Not only the choir, but every voice in the church, from the oldest to the youngest, rang out in perfect timing and harmony. Even though the same song was sung every Sunday, we never grew tired of it, because it sounded so pretty and no one even had to look in the hymn book for the words, because we knew them all by heart—all four verses.

During morning service, all of the children sat beside their best friends (unless they were temporarily mad at each other and not speaking). I, like everybody else, would slip notes to my friends about some of everything, like who thought she was cute because she had on new shoes or finally got her hair straightened, or return love notes to some boy who wanted to be my boyfriend with the "yes" or "no" box checked. We would go to the bathroom unnecessarily just to talk like we really wanted to, and if we felt brave enough, we would take turns sneaking in the dining room to see what was in all the different family food baskets, while someone looked out to see if anybody else was coming.

As long as we didn't get too loud or knew how to be extra sneaky, we usually got away with whatever we did, but there were certain people whom we had to watch for. The most important, for obvious reasons, was our parents. Then came the ushers. You see, the church we went to had those mean ushers who took their jobs *very* seriously. At that time, I actually thought the only job of an usher was to correct children for talking and playing in church. Sometimes we would rather have been caught by our parents than by the ushers, because at least that way, we would have only had to answer to our parents. If the ushers caught us, though, they would pinch or grab us so hard that it would nearly cut off our blood circulation, then report us to our parents after service, to be dealt with again. The last person we had to learn to watch for was the church mother, Mother Budd. Mother Budd had a special seat in front of the church. I thought this was because of the distinction of her being the church mother, and because she was so old that it would help her to see and hear in the church service better if she was seated up close. A few years later I found out that I was right about the first reason, but if the second reason was true, evidently Mother Budd didn't know it. During the whole service Mother Budd wouldn't look toward the front of the church but watched us instead. Anything that the ushers missed, Mother Budd would catch.

When morning service dismissed, the whole church buzzed with excitement. We children ran between the pews inside or up and down the church steps outside playing tag until our parents forced themselves away from their conversations long enough to make us stop. After we finished (or were made to stop) playing, we would discuss our plans for the rest of the day, which included eating dinner while waiting for the next service to begin.

When we stayed at church between services, Liz and I would play quiet games, read the Bible, get a hymn book and try to find the songs that the choir sang that morning, or go outside after being warned not to go too far. Sometimes we'd sneak to the store to spend the money that we were supposed to put in the church offering. Other times we'd play jacks or jump rope, but most of the time we'd start fighting, so Mom would make us come back in to take a nap until it was time for the next service. We would try so hard to stay out of trouble but rarely succeeded. The waiting was just too long.

Although our mom went through all the trouble of preparing our dinner every Sunday, sometimes Liz and I would go to the Wallace's house. It was totally different at the Wallace's. Gracie's older sister, Alma, was also Liz's best friend. Her younger sister, Joy, was only a few years older than Clarita, so the three of us were equally anxious to visit the Wallace's house whenever we had the opportunity. There was always something to do over there, whether it was going outside to climb trees, play ball, jump rope, or play with the many pets that they had. I remember a dog, a cat, a guinea pig, a rabbit, and a turtle, but I'm almost sure that there were even more. Although it was old and rusty, they even had a swing set.

When the weather was too bad, we stayed inside but still had just as much fun. Alma could play the piano. We'd all gather around this great big ole dusty piano (the kind with the real high back) and sing. Sometimes we were serious when we sang songs that we learned in the junior choir, or when Alma would try to show us how to play a song. Other times, when Gracie's mom wasn't paying attention to what we were doing, we got silly and copied how other people at church sung, testified, or shouted when they "got happy."

There was only one time when the Wallaces did something that totally shocked me. First of all, we didn't live in the same neighborhood as they did. They lived in the same neighborhood as the church, so the only time we spent any length of time with them was on Sundays. During the week, they hung out with the kids in their own neighborhood, just like we did. One time the kids in their neighborhood began picking on us for no other reason than the fact that they were bored and didn't know us that well. This was a fairly common practice for children of our age, I guess, but what shocked me so much was that the Wallaces joined in with them! I wouldn't have been surprised in the least if Tawanna Monk had done something like this, but *never* Gracie Wallace! Although Gracie and Alma never said anything, they still walked with the crowd close behind us, who continued to call us names and threaten to beat us up. Liz and I just kept walking, both of us too scared to turn around and say anything. I'm more than sure that Liz could've taken them on if they fought her one by one, but even Liz wasn't brave enough to mess with a crowd.

Thankfully, Jr. happened to be home on leave from the navy and was standing in the churchyard talking to a few church members. When he looked up the street and saw us coming back to the church with the crowd behind us, he immediately sensed that something was wrong. He came to meet us and told the kids to leave us alone, but they weren't ready to.

"I said leave them alone!" Jr. yelled.

"You can't make us!" one of the kids yelled.

"Yeah, you can't tell us what to do! You're not our father!" another kid yelled.

"We're not scared of *you* either!" yelled another kid's voice from the crowd.

While Jr. continued to argue with the kids, one of them ran home and got his dog. It was a big dog, too. I was terrified, but luckily, Jr. wasn't. He looked around him till he found a big stick.

"Let him go," Jr. ordered, ready to beat the life out of the dog. The boy kept talking trash, but he never did let that dog go.

That afternoon when the Wallaces came back to church, it was like nothing had ever happened.

The afternoon service was never too long or

boring, because there was no preaching most of the time. We mainly just sung, had youth programs like Easter and Christmas plays, Vacation Bible School closings, Sunday School promotions, Appreciation services, and things like that.

This was also the service during which my mom sang lots of times with a small group with called the Gospelets. Mom sang soprano and also sometimes played the piano for the group. The women also had about three or four different outfits just alike, so they looked almost as pretty as they sounded. I think that they could have easily been famous had the right strings been pulled. Years later I asked my mother whatever happened to that group. She told me that our pastor in Cleveland felt that it was too much for her to sing in the choir *and* sing in the group, so when she got out of the group, it gradually just fell apart. Mom wasn't actually the leader of the group, but all of the members were so close that they didn't want to go on without each other, so it probably would've been the same way if any one of the other women was first to leave.

I can imagine our pastor in Cleveland telling my mom that, because I do remember him being very strict. Mom told me about all the things they weren't allowed to do, like attend sporting events, or wear pants, sandals, or even blouses with short sleeves. She even told me that at the beginning of each school year, the pastor wrote a letter to all of the schools that the girls of the church went to asking that they be excused from gym. I guess this killed two birds with one stone: the sports and the girls wearing pants. Years later my brother told me about how he wanted to play baseball so bad, but my mom wouldn't let him because of the rules of the church. He said a few times he skipped choir rehearsal to go play baseball, because that was the only way that he ever got to play.

Liz sung a lot of solos in this service, too. (To this day she has an awesome voice—kind of a cross between Gladys Knight and Oleta Adams.) I asked my mom about the first time she realized that Liz could sing like that. She said that one day when she was about five years old and coloring in her coloring book, Liz just broke out and started singing "The Lord's Prayer." Mom said her voice was so clear and strong for a five-year-old that it was almost scary. She immediately tried to figure out a way to convince Liz to sing in church, but she had to be careful, because even at that young age, Liz was so contrary.

"Where'd you learn that song from, Liz?" Mom asked. Liz, never excited too much about anything even to this day, never looked up from the coloring book.

"My schoolteacher taught it to me."

"Would you sing it in church?" Mom carefully asked.

"Yes," Liz surprisingly answered.

Mom said Liz did sing it in church; she was so little that they stood her on a box so everyone could see her. The whole church went wild, and she's been singing ever since.

I also remember playing "Faith of Our Fathers" on my Autoharp on one of these programs. I was so nervous. Not because I was afraid I would mess up on the Autoharp, but because this was while Mitchell Nathane was my boyfriend and I couldn't decide if him being there or him not being there would make me feel better.

It was getting closer to my turn, and he wasn't there yet. Right before I was called, Mitchell came and sat in the row right in front of me, turned around, and looked in my eyes.

"You played that thing yet?" I just looked down and shook my head no. I was so nervous. After I played, the church gave me a standing ovation, but I only looked at Mitchell. The smile on his face was priceless. After service, everyone was asking me questions about the Autoharp, because it wasn't one of the more popular instruments and a lot of people had never seen one. I felt so important.

When afternoon service was over, we took a short break before Y.P.H.A. started. Y.P.H.A. stood for Young People's Holy Association and was mainly for the youth (and young at heart, of course) to come together for Bible lessons, fun and games, planned outings, and interaction with youth departments at other churches.

During the Y.P.H.A. sessions, we would separate into classes like we did for Sunday school; then afterward, we would all join together for the fun and games. My favorite game was the Bible Quiz, where a person would call out a book from the Bible, the chapter, and the verse and then everyone playing would race to find it. The first one to stand and read it out loud got a point. Although the little children could never find the verses as fast as the older children and ended up dropping out of the game early, we still enjoyed cheering for whom we wanted to win. There was a prize for the people who won the games and then we all had refreshments.

Night service was very similar to morning service, with the singing, preaching, offerings, and the whole nine yards. Sometimes during night service, other pastors would visit from other churches with their choirs and congregations, and sometimes we would visit other churches. I couldn't figure out if the sermons seemed so long because I was so sleepy, because I was too young to know what the preachers were talking about, or because the preachers were just long-winded. A few of the older children would stay up during this service to talk and play as they did in the morning service, but I could never stay awake for the entire night service. Never.

By the time Aunt Mary would take us back home, it would be about 11:00 P.M. So, you see, we were in church all day, and this was, without exaggeration, *every* Sunday.

Chapter 6

"All right, let's get started." I rose from the couch, collecting the breakfast trash and piling it into the bag in which it had arrived. I wasn't sure if Gloria had enjoyed the church service program or not, but I had certainly enjoyed it. There were a few times that I heard her comment "Amen," "That's right," or "You betta preach!"

"I guess I'll go in here and start on the kitchen." Gloria rose from the couch, stretching her limbs as far out as they would go. "Where your cleaning stuff?" she asked, peering into a few nearby boxes.

"Check that box right there on the dining room table." I pointed. "It's somewhere over there."

"Cut some music on." Gloria instructed even though she headed for the radio herself and plugged it in. With a few twists of the knob, she stopped at the old and new school R&B station, popped her fingers a few times to a Frankie Beverly jam, then began running water in the kitchen sink.

I spun around in a complete circle looking at all that needed to be done but not exactly knowing where to start. Terra had fallen asleep on top of the covers in the middle of the floor and had started to snore lightly. "I'm going to start in Terra's room; I can probably knock that out the fastest."

"All right, well, let's set a time limit for each room. That will help us make sure we get it all done. An hour should be good, right?"

"Sounds good." With my foot, I pushed a box labeled "school clothes" down the narrow hallway and into Terra's room. As I lifted garments out of the box, I was reminded of how badly she needed new clothes for school. That girl was growing up so fast it was hard for me to believe it although it was happening right before my very eyes. And kids were so cruel; if I didn't keep Terra styled in the latest fashion trends, it cost her days of merciless teasing. The days that she came home in tears telling me how her peers would poke fun at her would break my heart, but with my limited income, what could I do? Her daddy, with his no good self, wasn't making any kind of contribution in her life, financial or otherwise, which just made me angry every time I thought about it. Subconsciously I began to slam the dresser drawers shut as I put her clothes inside. I couldn't help but think of my own schooltime woes.

I dreaded walking to school on Monday mornings after the weekend. It wasn't that I didn't like school; in fact, I really loved it. On the way to school, though, Tawanna and I would walk together enjoying each other's friendship, laughing, chatting, and discussing in detail what had happened on the latest episode of *Dark Shadows,* our favorite soap opera.

Everything would be fine until about halfway between Tawanna's house and the school, when we'd make a stop at another classmate's, Janice's, house. This is when it got to the part that I dreaded. Janice was light skinned and freckle faced. From the time Janice came out of her house, Tawanna seemed to change. Nothing I said was funny anymore and whenever there was laughter, it was directed more *at* me rather than with me. Janice and Tawanna had more to share because their mothers were also friends, so they also saw each other on the weekends instead of just during the week. They'd talk about their hair appointments they went to that Saturday and how they didn't like to get perms because they burned, or about the movie they went to that Sunday. I could never contribute to these conversations, because I had never been to the movies and I didn't even know what a perm was, so I walked the rest of the way to school in silence while Tawanna and Janice chattered on.

I can't remember too many other everyday incidents that happened in school, but one day after school I saw something that I will never forget. I've seen a lot of mean things since then, but if I had to name the top three meanest things I've ever seen in life, this definitely would be among them.

There was a crowd of kids making a whole lot of noise and looking at something in the middle of the crowd. These kids were older than I was; they seemed to have been between sixth and eigth graders and because I was so much shorter than they were, it was hard for me to see. I thought about just not worrying about it and going home, because I had been warned by my father not to follow fights.

This couldn't have been a fight, though, because the crowd was closed so tightly and nobody was moving. Everybody was just standing still and making a lot of noise. I kept going around the crowd until I finally found a spot where I could see what was going on.

In the middle of the crowd was a boy and girl kissing on the mouth, but not because they wanted to. Behind the boy who was kissing was another boy. He didn't seem any older than the boy who was doing the kissing, but he was a whole lot tougher. The boy in the back was pressing his hand against the head of the boy who was kissing. Behind the girl who was kissing was a rougher-looking girl doing the same thing to her. These bullies, who were making the couple kiss, were actually leaning with their full body weight on their hands to push the couple's faces together. The kissing couple's eyes were closed tightly and their faces were soaking wet with tears.

I stood and stared in disbelief. How could they possibly be so mean? There was no telling how long they had made them do it before I was able to see them, but after I could see what they were doing, I was sure about two or three minutes passed before they stopped. Two or three minutes is a long time to kiss someone you *really love*, much less a total stranger whom you're being forced by bullies to kiss in front of a jeering crowd!

After the bullies got bored with what they were doing, they just stopped and walked away like it was no big deal. I didn't know why, but for some reason, as the crowd broke up, I found myself following the girl, who was still crying and had started to suck her thumb. I wanted so much to say something to her, but I wasn't sure of what to say. Eventually, she turned and looked at me, and although not a word was spoken, we seemed to have had a whole conversation with our eyes.

I'm so sorry they made you do that. I thought that it was so mean, my eyes said.

I know, but what could I do? the girl's eyes said.

I don't know and even though I wasn't part of it, I'm still sorry, my eyes answered.

Equipped with an electric drill, I quickly assembled the pieces to Terra's bed, then dragged her box spring and mattress across the room and placed them on the frame. Her *Dora the Explorer* sheet set and comforter were crumpled in a pile in the corner, where I'd dumped them to put the bed together, but in seconds her bed was perfectly made. Although I was tempted to sit there and rest for a minute, I was distracted by the phone ringing from my bedroom and the kitchen.

"You want me to get that?" Gloria yelled from the front of the apartment.

"I got it," I answered as I lifted the cordless handset but tossed it back down once I saw that the call was coming from Terrell's mother's house. I just didn't have the patience to fool with that man today.

Our marriage had been short, with the ending being disastrous, as most marriages end. The phone kept ringing until I lost my patience and snatched it off the receiver.

"What!" I screamed.

"Ivy, please."

"I can't, Terrell. I can't do it anymore. I told you that this would happen and you didn't believe me."

"But, Ivy, can you just listen to me for a minute?"

"Listen to what? To you tell me how sorry you are and how you are never going to do this again? How many times can you tell that same lie, Terrell, and expect me to believe it? What else can you possibly say to me that you haven't said ten times before?"

"Ivy, just please hear me out this one last time; after that, you don't ever have to speak to me again," he pleaded. "Please; I'm begging you."

I didn't want to, but I figured that maybe he would say something that would lead to me finally convincing him that it was really over.

"Go ahead, Terrell," I snapped, then sucked my teeth.

"Ivy, I swear to God—"

"How many times did I tell you that you're not supposed to do that?" I was in enough trouble with God all by myself; I didn't need him adding on to it. As he began to explain, I walked over to my front door.

"Oh yeah, you right. But look, Ivy, if you just give me one more chance, I—" The sound of me pounding on my own front door cut him off midsentence. "Who's that?"

"I gotta go." Gloria peered around the corner, but I dismissed her with a wave of my hand, then brought a finger to my lips motioning for her to keep silent.

"Ivy, who at your door?"

"I gotta go," I repeated and hung up the phone. Immediately it started to ring again and I turned the ringer off. I hadn't meant to, but I had awakened Terra. She stretched her little body upward and rubbed her eyes.

"Ma, who is that?" she asked through a yawn.

"Nobody. Do you want to go outside?" That pretty much was all I had to say to Terra, other than it was mealtime, to get her up and going.

"Yes!" She beamed, suddenly becoming lively as if she'd been up all day.

"Well, go brush your teeth and wash your face again while I find you some play clothes to put on." Inside of ten minutes, Terra was bounding for the door and across the small parking lot to a playground where a few other children were playing. I watched her from the living room window for the next several minutes as she got settled into a swing and began to fiercely pump her legs, taking to the sky. As I watched, I remembered a few of the children with whom I'd played outside.

I never played too long, though, because they all seemed to be so mean to me. I think this was because I was never a good fighter, so I was an easy target. Especially by the other children who were just as cowardly as I was and were happy to finally find someone whom they could get away with picking on.

I specifically remembered a time when I wanted to have my own swing set. I remember always thinking that when I finally got one, I wouldn't care whether I had anybody else to play with or not. Almost every day, I got Mom's Sears catalog and chose the one that I wanted. . . .

There wasn't a lot of grass in the front yard and no one in my neighborhood had a big backyard, so most of the time we all played together on the street. Before we started playing together, we "sealed" the game by crossing our arms, holding hands, and chanting

"Criss cross, applesauce,
nobody else can play with us,
for if they do, I'll take my shoe
and knock 'em till they're black and blue!"

The houses were very close together if not directly side by side. We mostly rode our bikes, skated, played jacks, or jumped rope. The smaller girls jumped rope the plain way and the older girls played double Dutch, but I could double Dutch just as good as anybody, so they had no problem letting me play with them unless Liz said I couldn't.

Then there were the "advanced" patty-cake games. My favorites were "Have you ever, ever, ever, in your long-legged life . . ." and "My father went to sea, sea, sea . . ."

When we played hide-and-seek, we decided who would be "it" by everyone putting their feet together and one person pointing to each foot while repeating:

"Engine, engine number nine,
going down Chicago line.
If the train jumps off the track,
do you want your money back?"

(Of course, everybody said yes—even in the sixties we didn't let anybody play with our money!)

"Y-E-S spells yes, so you are not it."

The person whose foot was being pointed to took his or her foot out and we continued until there was only one foot left. That person was "it."

Then there was the famous:

"Eeni meeni miney mo,
catch a nigger by his toe.
If he holler let him go,
eeni meeni mini mo."

While we were playing this game it was the only time we used the word *nigger* so loosely. Sometimes we'd even call ourselves a nigger when we were about to fight, chanting:

"You can roll yo' eyes, you can stomp yo' feet,
But this one black nigger you sho' can't beat!"

But if someone else called us a nigger, we'd quickly get them told:

"I'm not a nigger, I'm a Ne-gro,
when I become a nigger, I'll let you know!"

We had poems for some of everything.

Believe it or not, my favorite part of being outside was when my father and I sat on the porch together. He smoked cigarettes and I don't know if he came out to keep from smoking in the house, but I enjoyed sitting with him. He told me jokes, showed me tricks, and sang silly songs. Sometimes we'd walk to the store together and he'd buy us things to snack on while we were sitting on the porch, like ice cream, butter cookies, and cheese (I thought this was a strange combination initially, but it was actually really good), or "nabs." My father was the first, and for a long time, the only person whom I heard call small packages of cookies or crackers "nabs." I was full grown before I found out that they were called that because the first company to make them was Nabisco.

Those were the best of times, just enjoying the evening outside with my daddy. I missed him dearly. It was too bad that as far as I could tell, Terra would never have memories like those to look back on.

If Terrell could just pull himself together, then I wouldn't feel like I needed to keep his daughter away from him. Well, actually I wasn't keeping her away; I don't think I could really ever do that, because I knew the value of growing up with the love and support of family. I would want the same thing for my baby, but Terrell had just become so unglued that he kept himself away. It would do more harm than good for Terra to see him in his current condition, and under the circumstances, what else could I do?

Chapter 7

Both my parents' families were from North Carolina, but before too long, Momma's family relocated to Virginia, so those were our two choices each year for summer vacation.

When we would go to Virginia to visit my mother's family, we would take a Greyhound bus, which was fun, although it seemed like we would never get there. Momma would fill that same red food bag with chicken sandwiches, cake, fruit, and sodas. Knowing the goodies that were in it, the three of us kids would claim to be hungry before the bus could barely make it around the first corner.

When we would finally get to Virginia, my grandfather would meet us at the bus station in his taxicab and take us to his house to stay. We would stay at my grandmother and grandfather's house, but we would visit our other aunts' houses almost every day. My favorite aunt was my Aunt May, who had a twin sister, Aunt Faye.

Aunt May had two sons, Raymond and Timothy; she had a house full of beautiful furniture, and always had good food to eat. She was a nurse and a kitchen beautician, so we could expect to get our hair straightened while we were there. I hated it, because my hair was so long and thick and I was also very tender headed, especially when she got back to my "kitchen."

The only thing I didn't like about Aunt May's house is that she always had a big dog. One in particular that I remember was named Blackie. It seemed that everyone could get close to him except me. I was terrified of him and all my cousins thought that it was so funny.

Aunt Faye's house was totally different. Although she had four girls, they were all closer to Liz's age, so they wouldn't have too much to do with me. I was too little to play with or even talk to them most of the time.

Aunt Faye kept a dog all the time too. Even though he was a much smaller dog than Aunt May's, it made things even worse for me because he was kept in the house. I was miserable all summer because at Aunt May's, I was afraid to go outside and at Aunt Faye's, I was afraid to stay inside.

My mom's other sister, Aunt Gladys, was the meanest one. She didn't have any children and didn't seem to regret it in the least. She traveled a lot because her husband was in the military. They had a big dog too. Aunt Gladys liked it when people were afraid of her dog because it was her watchdog.

"Watchdogs are *supposed* to be mean and scare people! Whoever heard of a nice watchdog?" she'd say.

My mom's two brothers who lived in Virginia were Uncle Ed and Uncle Willie. Uncle Ed was the funniest one, and Uncle Willie was the meanest one. He was even meaner than Aunt Gladys, which was very hard to be.

My mom's youngest brother, Uncle Nate, was also my godfather. He lived in Ohio, like we did, only in a different city.

Even though there were plenty of houses that we could've visited while in Virginia, I was pretty much satisfied with just staying home with Grandma. She cooked the best-tasting foods! Breakfast would be something as simple as biscuits, fatback, molasses or Karo syrup, and milk. The sound of this combination is far different from the taste, trust me. I don't remember too much about lunch, but oh, those dinners! I'm telling ya'll, the momma on *Soul Food* had nothing on my grandma, especially on Sundays.

Grandma loved the beach. I remember lots of times she packed a lunch and took us to two different beaches. Sometimes she would collect all my cousins and other times she'd just take Liz and me. We liked one of the beaches better than the other one, because there were rides, games, and lots of food to buy there. Sometimes Grandma gave us money for the rides and games, but hardly ever for the food.

"They too high!" she would say with a frown on her face. Then she'd pull out the lunch that she packed, which by this time was cold if it was supposed to be hot, or warm if it was supposed to be cold. I wonder what she would have to say about the prices of refreshments at the amusement parks today!

My personal favorite ride was the Black Widow Spider. Everybody else's was the bumper cars. My least favorite was the fun house. Till this day I can't figure out why they named it that. Even though most people do have "fun" when they go in there, it still never seemed to me that the name was quite right, because it was so dark and scary.

There wasn't as much to do at the other beach Grandma took us to because they only had picnic tables and swings, which the children weren't too nice about sharing. Liz and I blended in with them sometimes, but most of the time we didn't. We usually just ended up playing with each other (or fighting), while my grandmother sat on the sand or walked along the beach alone. Every so often I would look for her and spot her by her hat. It was always a wide-brimmed straw hat with flowers going around it, or a long scarf on it that hung down her back.

Summer vacations in North Carolina with my father's family were a little different; there weren't as many cousins there to play with, because I only had one uncle, Uncle James, who lived there. Although he had five children, none were close to my age, but they were overall nicer than my Virginia cousins.

In Ohio, there was a lot of pavement, and in Virginia, there was a lot of grass, which dictated the way we played as kids, but in North Carolina there was neither. There was only a lot of dirt, gravel, and asphalt, so I can't even remember really playing there. All I do remember is frequently sitting on the front porch eating lots of watermelon, shooing flies, and playfully talking about each other.

The very worst thing about North Carolina was that my uncle had no indoor plumbing. The water tasted funny, because it was drawn from a well, and when we went to the bathroom, it was in the outhouse in the backyard. I cried whenever I had to go, because I hated it so much. There were so many bugs, flies, or spiders crawling around out there and the stench was unbearable.

The second worst thing about spending the summer in North Carolina was being made to go over to Uncle James's mother-in-law's house. This lady had to be the meanest lady in the world, more than Aunt Gladys and Uncle Willie combined. She had two young children named Bobbi and John who were just as mean as she was.

I remember we had to get up at the crack of dawn to go over to the lady's house while Uncle James and his wife went to the fields to pick tobacco. Other than dip snuff, the woman would cook the nastiest food. The worst of all was the squash, and it seemed like she cooked it every day for breakfast, lunch, and dinner. Liz and I were continually threatened with a whipping if we didn't eat it, which only resulted in us holding it in our mouths to later spit it in the well . . . which would explain why the well water tasted so terrible. I'm sure that we weren't the only ones throwing things in there that didn't belong. Come to think of it, Momma told me that one time when she was a little girl drawing water from that same well, somebody brought up a drowned cat.

Once when we were over at Bobbi and John's, I had to go to the bathroom but was scared to go in the outhouse by myself. Bobbi volunteered to go with me, but only for her own selfish intentions. While I was using the bathroom, she started digging in the corner of the outhouse with a long stick. All of a sudden about a hundred of those spiders with the real long legs came out. That was the only time I remember running faster than Bobbi.

Remember, Liz didn't take a lot of mess so they didn't mess with her too much. Sometimes she would take up for me, but only if she wasn't mad with me too. I do remember Liz getting in deep trouble one time while we were over there, though, for dipping some snuff. Now that I think about it, Liz got in trouble more because of whom the snuff belonged to than for actually dipping it.

My very best memory of North Carolina was my second boyfriend. William, whose nickname was Screwball, was cute with a big Afro. I can remember sitting on the sliding board of the swing set in front of my uncle's house and William was standing beside me caressing my arm and looking deep into my eyes while "La La Means I Love You" by the Delphonics played softly on the radio. Although I couldn't have been any more than eleven and much too young to know what real love was, I was sure that it was what I was experiencing at that time. I wish I could have frozen that moment; love was so simple, innocent, and painless then.

Chapter 8

Things were coming together much quicker than I thought. Terra's room was completely done, including her wall hangings, desk, and closet. It looked like she had been occupying the room for two years.

Gloria had put away all the dishes and food and had even started baking some chicken and boiling macaroni elbows to make her famous macaroni and cheese. She was working through the dining room when I entered the kitchen, drawn by the smell.

"That had to be Terrell on the phone a while back."

"It sure was, girl. I don't have time for his mess today. Mattafact, how he get this number? I haven't even been here a full seventy-two hours yet."

"Well, you know what they say: where there's a will, there's a way," she commented as she sprayed my glass tabletop with window cleaner and wiped it down with crumpled newspaper. "I just hope he don't come over here acting a fool."

"He has better sense than that," I responded, sorting through a box of DVDs and VHS tapes. "He knows I will call the cops in a minute." Taking a seat on the floor in front of the entertainment center, I began sliding the movies alphabetically in their appropriate slots. It would take me a few extra minutes instead of just stuffing them in the cabinets any kind of way, but organized was how I liked things.

No sooner than I reached for the phone and pushed the ringer switch back to the "on" position did it ring right in my hand, this time displaying an out-of-state number.

"Hey, Ma." *Lord, have mercy,* I thought. I could hear the distress in my oldest daughter Michelle's voice right away.

"Hey, baby. How you doing?" I should've known better than to ask.

"Ma . . ." Her voice had in an instant become more shaky. This wasn't the first time since she'd been away that she had called home to cry on my shoulder.

"What is it now, Michelle?"

"Can I *please* come home? *Please* . . ." she begged. That girl hadn't been gone a full two months, but she'd called begging to come home at least three other times. She'd left anxious and excited about both starting college and spending time with her dad, who was a professor at Florida State University, which is where she attended college. Because of his state residency there, both Michelle and my son Michael were able to take advantage of in-state tuition rates, not to mention other discounts that weren't offered to students whose parents weren't employed as school faculty.

"Michelle, I really want you to stay there." I knew she was only suffering from a mild case of homesickness.

"But, Ma, I hate it here. Please, Ma . . ."

"You know what, Michelle? I really don't understand you. Do you know what kind of an opportunity you're ready to walk away from? Do you know how many people would love to have that same opportunity?" I don't know how many times I had said this to her before, but just like all the other times, she wasn't trying to hear what I was saying.

"But, Ma, it's a lot of people that make it without going to college. All they have to do is stay in one job and move up. Look at Aunt Liz. . . ." Liz had gotten an entry-level job for the city practically right out of high school and had been there ever since, receiving promotion after promotion.

"Yeah, but like I told you before, why would you want to start at the bottom when you can get a college degree and come in at the top or at least in the middle, Michelle? Do you know how many kids want to go to college and can't go?" Silence. "I've never told you anything wrong, and I'm telling you, what you have is priceless." More silence. I hid my exasperation. "I'll talk to you again soon, okay? Call any time you want to talk." Continued silence. This meant she was in tears and couldn't form any words. "I love you."

I actually understood Michelle's plight, having lived through a relocation experience, although I was much younger. I guess it didn't really matter how old you were, though; moving away from everything familiar to you to start all over again in a new place was always hard.

* * *

"We're moving to Virginia," Momma announced. Her tone spoke in finality, not that I would have verbally questioned her. I just stood there in shock as the emotions lined up and started talking to me again. "Your granddaddy is real sick and I need to be there to help Momma."

That was it. End of discussion. He had cancer, which at that time was a word automatically associated with death. Next thing I knew, we were on the road with all of our belongings . . . except my father. It wasn't made privy to me as to why he wasn't coming; he just didn't come. And that was the last time we all lived together under the same roof.

Mom took Liz and me with her to the hospital to visit Grandaddy every day. My aunts also took their children with them. Because we were all too little to go to his room, Liz and I would sit in the hospital lobby with our cousins. Almost immediately after we greeted each other, the tormenting would begin. First, we would all go get something from the snack machine located in the basement.

"Ivy, look right there. See that door?" Timothy once started.

"Yeah, what about it?"

"Guess what's in there."

I shrugged my shoulders nonchalantly. "Don't know and don't care," I answered, digging my fingers in a bag of barbeque potato chips.

"That's where they keep the dead people," he said in his most haunting voice, stretching his eyes as wide as he could.

"Uh-uh!"

"Yes, they do, and my momma told me that if you make too much noise down here, the dead people will wake up and take you in the room with them!" he added.

"No, they won't!" I said, although I was totally horrified.

"Uh-huh! You know my momma work here, so she would know. Plus I know you ain't calling my momma a liar," he challenged. I gulped in double fear—fear that what he was saying was true, and fear that he would go running to Momma and Aunt May claiming that I'd called her a liar. The punishment for that could be far worse than being dragged into a room by the living dead.

"We better go back upstairs," I suggested, trying to change the subject. "Momma and them probably looking for us." Knowing that our mothers didn't play, we all headed to the elevators. With the fear of the dead behind me, we coasted back to our floor, but just as I was about to step out of the elevator, Timothy pushed me back inside and quickly pushed the button that would send the car back to the basement before he hopped off in hysterical laughter. The elevator coasted back to the basement and I was down there alone, scared to death, terrified that the slightest little move I made would be enough to conjure up a slew of bodies. I stood in the elevator perfectly still until I got myself together enough to ever so carefully lift my hand to push the first-floor button, relieved when the elevator doors slid shut again and the car lifted from the basement. When the door opened, they were all standing there bursting at the seams in laughter.

Now if that is how I was treated by my own flesh and blood, you can only imagine how my friends in the street would treat me from time to time.

Momma, Liz, Clarita, and I moved into a big house right next door to my grandma and granddad. Our house had a big front porch that went all the way across the front of it, and the yard space in the back and between my and my grandmom's house was bigger than we'd ever had before or since. I immediately made friends with the girl who lived next door, on the other side of our house, Freda, and with the girl who lived across the street, Nicky.

The first topic of our conversation was my accent.

"You talk so funny. Why you say stuff like that?"

"Like what?"

"When you talk about both of us, you say 'you all.'"

"Well, what am I *supposed* to say?"

"We just say 'ya'll.'"

"Oh."

"And then when we ass you to do something that you don't want to do, you say 'no.'"

"That's because I don't want to do it."

"Then just say 'ain't.'"

"'Ain't'?"

"Yeah, 'ain't.'"

"What does that mean?"

"It means 'I'm not.'"

"Then why don't you just say that?"

"Because it takes too long to say when you can just say one word, 'ain't.'"

"Oh. Well, why do you all say 'ass'?"

"Awww! We ain't say no 'ass,' girl. That's a bad word!"

"You say it all the time when you say, 'Let me ass you something' or 'You got something to ass me'. You said it just a minute ago."

"Well, when you say 'ass' and you talking a question and not your butt, it's not a bad word." Everything would get quiet and then we'd all bust out laughing.

Of course I had heard this kind of talking before from visiting Virginia and North Carolina every summer, but it hadn't dawned on me yet that now that I actually lived down South, I was supposed to talk like this, too.

Freda, the girl who lived next door, was a tomboy, because she had a whole lot of brothers. Nicky, the girl across the street, was spoiled rotten, because she was an only child. Nicky wore the cutest little shorts sets with different colored tennis shoes to match every one of them.

They taught me how to do cartwheels. I taught them how to double Dutch. They taught me how to do handstands. I taught them how to skate. When we got bored, we climbed the trees in my grandma's backyard for apples. Grandma had two apple trees, a little vegetable garden, and a grapevine, so we were always snacking on something from her backyard.

"Ya'll better git down out that tree 'fore ya'll fall and break ya necks!" Grandma would yell through the screen door at us. "Why don't ya'll just git the ones on the ground?" We never wanted to do that, because it wasn't as fun as climbing, and besides, the ones on the ground had those ugly, soft, brown spots on them from starting to rot. We even saw some with worms actually coming out of them. Before I moved to Virginia, I thought that this was something that was only in pictures.

As soon as we were settled in our house, we went to our new church. It didn't take long to find one because our pastor in Cleveland suggested a church in Virginia to Momma before we left.

This church was much smaller than the church we came from in Cleveland, and initially, the people weren't too friendly. Momma said several times that she wouldn't have stayed there had it not been for the pastor, Bishop Edison, and about two other people in the church. The other people who went there just didn't make her feel welcome.

The senior choir was small and sounded really bad. Liz and I laughed at them so hard that Momma had to sit between us. They had no junior choir and the kids weren't exactly mean to us, just very stuck-up.

There was only one person who warmed up to me almost instantly, and to this day she is still a warm person. Even though Mildred was only twelve, like I was, she was different from other twelve-year-olds. She kind of put me in mind of Gracie Wallace with her kindhearted ways. I can't remember one time when she said something bad about somebody, even when a person didn't treat her fairly.

After morning service, Mildred and I sometimes

went home with each other for dinner. I eventually started going home with other children too, just like they started coming home with me. (That was the thing then—who was going home with whom after church. It really got on our parents' nerves, because we never checked with them first. We just made plans among ourselves like we were running things, sometimes up to a whole month in advance.) I liked Mildred's house the best, because she had a lot of sisters and brothers. I think there were eight of them altogether. Our friendship outlasted all the others I made when I first came to the church, and even today, she is a very dear friend of mine. It's surprising when I tell people that we've been friends for as long as we have. Sometimes, we ourselves are even surprised when we think of how long it's been.

The best part I liked about the church when we first got there, though, believe it or not, was the preaching. I think Bishop Edison was older than our pastor in Cleveland, but he was much younger at heart. He used words in his sermons that were much easier to understand, and after church he passed out candy to the children.

Soon after we started going there, the church held some kind of youth program after the Sunday morning service. It was very unorganized, nothing like the programs we had at our church in Cleveland. When the person in charge would call on somebody to do something, the person called on would do a whole lot of laughing and playing before they came up; that's if they came up at all. Then, when they did come up, they wouldn't do their best, but just laugh through whatever presentation they made. One time when this happened, Momma leaned over and whispered to Liz, "Don't you want to sing something?" Liz didn't even look back at her.

"No."

"Please sing, Liz," Momma pleaded softly. Liz finally agreed, and Momma wasted no time standing to her feet.

"My daughter would like to sing a song if it's okay." The entire congregation hushed into a silence.

As Liz went up to the front of the church, escorted by my Momma, who would accompany her on the piano, the entire sanctuary church was filled with curiosity. Liz never looked around at the congregation but stared straight ahead and started to sing in her rich and powerful voice:

> *"Who made the mountains?*
> *Who made the trees?*
> *Who made the rivers to flow to the seas?*
> *And who sends the rain when the earth is dry?*
> *Somebody bigger than you and I."*

After that, the people in the church started warming up to us a little more. A little later, a junior choir was formed, for which Momma played the piano and, of course, Liz led most of the songs.

School in Virginia was a hard adjustment, because the fourth graders were at a higher level than the fourth graders in Cleveland, In Cleveland, we were still adding and subtracting. I was the second smartest person in my class in math and reading. In Virginia, they were doing long division and learning to speak French.

They were also much too strict. The disciplinary measures they took were unbelievable, and it was the black children who seemed to get into the most trouble for the least little thing. Unfortunately (or so I thought at that time), I was a black child. When I say "trouble," I don't mean sent home with a note so that I could get into trouble with my mom. Lots of times, it didn't even get that far. What I mean is getting sent to the office to be paddled by the principal. I would rather have gotten it from my mom, because at least that way the whole school wouldn't have known.

I remember once when a girl was copying off my paper while we were doing math. I was trying not to let her, but I was afraid of her, so instead of just telling her to stop doing it, I kept moving my paper around so it would be hard for her to see it. Once when the teacher looked up, I had just put another answer down on my paper and looked at the girl's paper to see if she was going to write down the same answer. The teacher automatically assumed it was me who was copying the girl's paper and sent me to the office.

Another time we were playing outside at recess and I accidentally bumped into the teacher while running. Before I even got a chance to apologize, the teacher spun around and was screaming at me, accusing me of almost knocking her down. After the principle got finished with me, I wished that I had not only knocked her down, but helped her up and knocked her down again!

My favorite part of school was lunchtime. Before moving to Virginia, I had never heard of having a full hot-cooked meal at school for lunch. The school lunches seemed just like dinners to me. Even the vegetables were good. We could smell the bread baking while we were outside for recess. I could hardly wait for my teacher to hold up her hand, signaling our class to line up and go in to wash our hands and eat.

Finally, my grandfather was released from the hospital, but he still stayed in a hospital bed in the corner of the dining room when he got home. Momma visited frequently to help my grandma bathe and feed him, and Aunt May was there most of the time too; being a nurse, she knew a lot about what to do for him.

For the most part, we stayed out of the way, but whenever I did peek behind the curtain that had been strung up in the middle of the room, he seemed to be getting thinner and thinner. He looked so much different from the man who used to pick us up from the bus station in his taxicab while smoking his pipe. I didn't know it then, but later I learned that the hospital had pretty much sent him home to die.

The date was June 14, 1968. I was so happy because it was the last day of school, but when I got home no one was there. I went next door to my grandma's house and everybody was there: my mom, my aunts and uncles, and my cousins. Everybody was crying. Something was missing. I looked in the corner. The hospital bed was empty. My grandfather was gone. . . .

* * *

Interrupting my thoughts, Terra burst through the door, looking as if she had literally laid down on the ground and rolled over fifteen times. She tilted her head to the ceiling and sniffed a few times.

"Ma, I'm hungry again," she said, detecting the aroma of barbeque sauce and cabbage.

"We're going to eat in a few minutes, Terra; Miss Gloria is in the kitchen cooking right now. I finished your room while you were outside; go take a look at it . . . And don't sit on the bed with those dirty clothes on!" I yelled down the hall as I looked at her clothes and wondered how they got that way so quickly.

"Ooh, Ma! It look so pretty!" Terra's round face beamed brightly as she excitedly took in her surroundings. The furnishings and décor were all the same, but she seemed mesmerized by how things were positioned in her new room. "Can I watch a movie while Miss Gloria finish cooking?"

"After you take a bath." I helped her wriggle out of her play clothes and tossed them into her hamper. "Go ahead and start your water and get in the tub while I find the box that has the towels and washcloths in it. I'll be in there in a minute, okay?"

"Okay." She paused pensively, then looked up at me. "Ma?"

"Yes, baby?"

"Is Daddy coming later?" For a second my eyes fell to her belly, which protruded from the hem of her T-shirt.

"Not this time, Terra."

"Why not," she asked innocently.

"Daddy has to work on some things first," I vaguely explained.

"But I thought he didn't have a job anymore," she reasoned. "So how is he going to work?" Terra had no business knowing that Terrell was out of work again. I really needed to do a better job of managing my conversations around her.

"Well, Terra, that is one of the things that Daddy needs to work on—finding a place to work. And there are some other things that he needs to get better at first."

"My teacher said if you want to get better at something you have to keep practicing it over and over again," she contributed.

"That's right. If you work hard on something by practicing, pretty soon you'll get really good at it." *Spending your bill money on drugs included!* I thought.

"Well, I wish he was here 'cause I miss him."

I didn't know how to respond to that, so I simply said, "Go 'head and get in the tub, Terra. I'll be in with your washcloth in a minute."

I found Gloria in the living room going through a box labeled Home Interior. She had located my tool set and had pulled out the hammer and a small box of nails.

"How do you want this stuff arranged?" she asked, inspecting each wall, then looking down at the various pieces she'd laid on the floor and couch. Although I heard what she said, my response was delayed, for I was thinking about what Terra had just said to me. Gloria noticed my initial lack of response. "You all right?" She caught me smudging away a tear.

"Yeah, girl," I lied. Well, actually I didn't lie; in the whole scope of things, I was all right. "Just thinking . . ." I added. "Umm, you can put it up how you think it will look best." I waved my hand dismissively, freeing myself of that task, and began digging through the box of linens. I just couldn't focus on it right now. "I'll start on the linen closet."

As I pushed the box of linens down the hall, stopping by the bathroom to give Terra the items she needed, I shook my head as I thought of what my baby was going through and how similar it was to my own life. Even down to the very place I lived.

My new apartment was much more confining than the house we'd just moved from. That would be another transition for Terra to work through. Instead of having a huge yard and plenty of inside space with no shared walls, there was no yard and I had to be conscious that there was a neighbor beneath me who probably wouldn't take too kindly to Terra's running about. I promised myself that this wouldn't last too long, though. Every child needed a house and yard.

Chapter 9

Shortly after my grandfather passed, Momma moved us to an apartment complex, which was the first apartment in which I'd ever lived. Even though it didn't have the same privacies as a single-family home, I was excited because the apartments had been newly constructed. The houses that I'd lived in before, though large, had always been older, and less modern.

For the most part, all of the kids in the neighborhood were either bullies or had established friendships so tight with each other that they didn't want to be bothered with anybody else. I kept trying to "fit in" with the kids from the new neighborhood, but Liz didn't. She was more selective in her friendships or just made herself content with being alone.

Eventually, the other children in the neighborhood started to talk to me, but it wasn't to be friendly. It seemed to be a big deal to intimidate the "new kid on the block." I was so glad when someone new moved in the neighborhood, but the tables always turned back to me. This was mainly because they figured out that I wasn't a fighter and was very easily intimidated.

The meanest people on the block were the Prince family. Not all of the kids in the Prince family, just Teresa, the girl who was my age, and Ron, her brother, who was a couple of years older than me.

Ron and Teresa were *always* doing something they didn't have any business doing! Especially Teresa. She would have people mad at each other without even knowing why. She would do stuff like get someone to come to you and make believe he or she didn't like her or her mother. If you were stupid enough to agree with that person, he or she would go back and tell Teresa what *you* said. Then Teresa would approach you wanting to fight. She also stole like crazy, but if you were ever with her and she got caught, you would get the blame. I could never figure out why it was that whenever her mom or older brother sent her to the store, she would steal what they sent her after, keep the money, and buy candy. I could never figure out why she just didn't steal the candy.

Teresa's favorite thing was telling somebody else that I had said something about them so they'd want to fight me, because she knew how afraid I was to fight even though I was taller than everybody else in the neighborhood. I did try to learn to fight, but it seemed to me that fighting was a natural ability that I just didn't have.

There was always some kind of drama in our neighborhood. Almost every day, somebody was fussing or fighting and I was always somehow involved. Lots of times Liz would take up for me, even though during those times we could barely get along our-

selves. But you know how it went: you could pick on
your sisters and brothers all you wanted, but everybody else had better not. Thank God she was my
sister and my "curse" hadn't affected the fact that
blood was thicker than water.

One day *all* the neighborhood girls were after
me; again, behind something that Teresa Prince
had started. It had to have been at least a dozen girls
in our front yard, which was more than enough
reason for me to stay in the house and peek from
the window while they double-dog dared me to
come outside. When Liz figured out what was going
on, she grabbed the vacuum cleaner pipe. Liz wasn't
afraid of *nobody*.

"Come on here," she barked at me. I was scared
to death of going out there, but I didn't know who
I was more afraid of—the girls or Liz. I was pathetic.

Liz went outside and stood right in front of the
girls.

"Who out here messing with my sister *now?*" she
spat out while holding the pipe with one hand and
the other hand on her hip. All those girls together
could've easily taken Liz, but not one even spoke,
much less moved. I thought about the crowd from
the Wallace neighborhood in Cleveland many years
before then.

"I *thought* so," Liz said. Then she turned around
and went back in the house with me behind her
like a little puppy.

As soon as we got in the house, she started in
on me.

"Girl, you make me sick with your big, tall, scaredy-
cat, crybaby self. I don't know why you keep playing
with those girls. You know how they are."

"I know. I ain't playing with them no more," I lied. As soon as things cooled down, I was right back out there with them and being tormented again. You see, I may not have been a good fighter, but I just loved being around people, and as mean as they were, at that time they were the only people to be around.

There was only one time in particular when everybody in the neighborhood wanted to be Liz's "friend," even the people whom she clearly couldn't stand or who clearly couldn't stand her, which was just about everybody. Only one time. This was the time when Liz met The Jackson Five. She and one of her girlfriends saw them at a concert in Richmond and somehow got to go backstage to personally meet them. When Liz came back and told everybody, of course no one believed her, but luckily she and her girlfriend had made plans with the Jacksons to meet them again when they came to Norfolk, which was only a couple of weeks away. This time Liz came back with pictures. These weren't just pictures of large groups of people where Liz could've just *happened* to be around, these pictures included a picture of Liz and Jermaine, then another of Liz and Tito, then one more of Liz and Jackie—they were sitting on the bed in their hotel room.

I was so excited, I felt just like it had happened to me. I wanted the neighborhood girls to see them, but Liz didn't, and when one of them was bold enough to ask her, she had no problem letting her know.

"Hell no!" she'd yell as hard as she could.

Of course they talked me into letting them see the pictures when Liz wasn't home. I would let them see the pictures through the window, but I wouldn't bring those pictures outside. No way. I knew those girls too well and they'd probably snatch them from me and not give them back. I knew that if something happened to those pictures, I would be as good as dead.

Another time when we were all outside in front of our house fussing, Momma came outside and Ron started mouthing off at her. "What you lookin' at? Ain't nobody call you outside, nosy!" he said with his disrespectful self.

It wasn't such a general practice to discipline other people's kids anymore, or else Momma would have tore into his tail with a switch. Instead she warned, "If you don't get out of my yard, I'm going in the house and get some hot water just for you."

"Go 'head!" Ron called Mom's bluff, refusing to leave the yard. Less than a minute later Momma returned with the promised pot of hot water and doused Ron. As she slung the water in Ron's face, I held my breath. When he finished spitting and clearing his eyes, he looked as if he wanted to kill Momma.

"Don't you hit that lady, Ron!" his older sister yelled, reading Ron's mind.

With an expression of pure evil and anger he stood in place. "I should hit you, but my sister told me not to!" he growled.

I was praying that Momma would just go back in the house, because I knew how crazy that boy was, and as mad as he was, I'm sure that he would have put a hurtin' on my momma.

I often wonder what happened to the Prince family, especially Ron and Teresa. Last I heard, Teresa got married to a minister and Ron died of a drug overdose.

* * *

I remember one day at school I was teasing this girl because she was cockeyed. At first the girl didn't pay me any attention, but I kept rubbing it in and making people laugh at her by crossing my eyes like hers. Finally, the girl got tired of me and the next time I looked at her she gave me the "I'ma beat your tail after school" signal. Ya'll remember it—it was when someone made sure he or she had only your attention and then balled his or her fist up making sure you saw it. If the person went so far as to punch the inside of his or her other hand and didn't care who else saw it, you *knew* you were in for it. Anyway, as soon as the bell rang, the girl walked over to me and beat me good. I never have or will forget the beating that girl put on me. From that day on, I never talked about anybody else's eyes. Not to the person's face anyway.

Remembering how I was always so easily intimidated and afraid to fight like other children my age made me think that this was definitely part of my punishment for mouthing off to God the way I did so many years ago.

When I finally got tired of playing games with those mean girls in my neighborhood (or rather, got tired of letting them play games with me), I got very close with one girl who also lived on our block but hardly ever came outside. I guess Cindy knew how the other girls in the neighborhood were and preferred not to be bothered with them, or she just didn't mind being alone. We hit it off, and for the next four years, Cindy was my closest and dearest friend. We did everything together.

Her mom dressed her, her sisters, and her brother really nice, and because I was with Cindy all the time, it wasn't too long before I also started taking more pride in the way I dressed. I loved to go shopping with them. Lots of times we bought jeans and tops that were alike. Her very favorite store was Davey Jones Locker. Even when I didn't have money to buy anything, which was most of the time, Cindy would let me help her pick things out and later let me borrow them.

I ate dinner with her family a lot too, but my mom didn't like it when I did that, because sometimes we didn't have a lot of food at home and when I ate dinner with Cindy's family, my mom didn't think it was fair to Liz and Clarita. I couldn't understand this at first, but Mom promised me that when I had children of my own, I would. As Mom was about a lot of things, she was right.

"I sure appreciate you for coming over today, Gloria." Truly famished, we all took a seat at the dining room table. Gloria had actually set the table for the three of us and had the food in serving dishes. "You didn't have to go through this elaborate setup, though."

"Yes, I did. Girl, this is a celebration dinner for you. You're starting over, moving on, letting go of some drama and pulling it all together again. That is worthy of having the table set in your honor. Girl, we need to have a full-blown party!"

Now that she'd spelled it out like that, I had to

agree with her. "You're right," I said, half blushing. "Let's say grace." We joined hands and then I lead us in prayer, remembering to thank God not only for the food, but also for a great friend.

I was glad that the TV had been turned back on; Gloria and Terra watched an episode of *The Jeffersons,* while I remembered my first party.

Chapter 10

The year was 1971 and I was thirteen years old. This was the time that everybody had those good house parties, and on this particular night, Cindy and her two sisters were having one.

Cindy had two *fine* cousins who came around a lot, and that night when they came to the party, they brought their friend Butch. Along that time, we defined *fine* as being light skinned and having a big Afro and/or a "good" grade of hair. Almost nothing else mattered. If a guy had these two qualities, he was a shoo-in for being "fine." Although Butch didn't have these qualities, he was still mysteriously sexy. He was the tall, dark, and handsome type—the type who was slowly but surely gaining ground on the light-skinned guys with the big Afros.

I had on my red hot pants, a white blouse, white stockings, and my black Sunday shoes. My Afro was picked out as far as it would go and was complemented by a pair of large hoop earrings. I just *knew* I looked good.

Butch seemed to be automatically attracted to me.

Every time a slow song was put on, he asked me to dance. I had never slow dragged before this night, but it came very naturally with him leading me.

Time was moving much too fast. Momma had given us a time to be home, but when that time came, Liz and I weren't ready to leave. Pretty soon, Mom started calling over there. I kept one eye on Liz, who was in the corner with one of the "fine" cousins, while I continued to dance with Butch. Momma called a few more times, but Liz and I just kept watching each other, determined not to be the first one to pull away from what we were doing.

Michael Jackson started to sing "Maybe Tomorrow" as Butch held me closer and started to sing in my ear along with Michael. I had just closed my eyes and let myself get totally lost in the moment when Cindy tapped me on my back and whispered in my ear.

"Your momma's at the door."

"I gotta go," I blurted as I pulled away from Butch and glanced in the corner for Liz, who had already left. She must have left through the front door, because I never saw her pass me. I can't for the life of me figure out how she got out that fast. It was almost like she smelt danger coming like those animals on the Discovery channel or something.

I casually walked out the back door, where my mom was waiting. As soon as I passed her, I felt something cut me across my back. She started whipping me. I couldn't believe that my mom had actually come over there to whip us home! I took off running, and I never knew my mother could run as fast as I could, but she never stopped hitting me. At least that's how it felt, unless it was just the stings of shame that I was feeling. I had never been that embarrassed before, nor have I been since then.

The next day I asked Cindy had anyone laughed at us.

"No, they were talking about how wrong your momma was for doing that." That made me feel a little better. Only a little. Then she said something that totally threw me for a loop: "Butch was the only one laughing about it." Although I was deeply hurt because he laughed, he ended up being my boyfriend for the next three years.

Until this day, this incident bothers me even though if I haven't learned anything else from going to church all those years, I did learn that we have to forgive each other if we feel we've been wronged in any way because Christ forgives us. Although I knew that sooner or later I had to forgive my mom for doing this, it took me years to do it. I just didn't understand what the big deal was, because, first of all, she knew exactly where we were (which, by the way, was only four doors down!), and secondly, if she was *that* angry with us for not coming home when she called for us, she could've waited until we came home to whip us.

My mother told me a lot of things that I didn't understand when I was young, like I'm sure a lot of mothers also tell their children. Since I've been grown and had children of my own, I now understand why she said and did a lot of the things that she did at that time. What she did that night is the only thing that I've not been able to understand. No one could even pay me to ever embarrass my children like that. No one.

Anyway, Butch was my first real love. I think what I loved most about him was that he was so comical. Whenever we were together, we hung out in his neighborhood and it seemed that everybody knew and loved to be around him, especially when he started telling jokes and talking about people. He had this big, old-fashioned car that was black with a red interior and he kept that thing shining. He was the first one to take me to the movies. We went to see *Super Fly*. Boy was I in love with that boy. Little did I know, I had a lot to learn about love and relationships.

I was hanging out at Cindy's one afternoon when one of the cousins whom I'd met Butch through came by.

"Where's Butch?" I asked, thinking that they hung out together quite regularly.

"I'on't know; I ain't seen him today, but if you want to, I can take you to go look around for him," Eddie volunteered. I jumped at the opportunity. After all, I was in love.

Eddie drove around for about thirty minutes, checking all the spots where Butch usually hung out. When we couldn't locate him, he began taking me back to Cindy's.

"You heard that new song by The Isley Brothers?" he asked just as easily as a person asks for the time of day.

"Which one?"

"The one that says if you can't be with the one you love, love the one you with."

I was shocked that he would suggest such a thing, because he and Butch were so close. Again, I had a lot to learn.

* * *

A few years later, I managed to capture the attention of two college guys. The first one was tall, dark, handsome—had a beautiful body build—and played on the football team. He was a physical education major and went by the nickname of Chippy, probably because one of his front teeth was chipped, but strangely it gave him an even sexier smile. The other was a straight nerd. He was a political science major named Arthur.

Nevertheless, I couldn't be so bothered with either one of these guys, because I was too much in love with Butch. I took every chance that I could to be with him. For the very first time, I was really in love. Being with Butch made me feel that my childhood years were officially over . . . only to launch me into years of more "mature" drama.

Chapter 11

I'd been hanging clothes in my walk-in closet when Gloria walked in with the cordless phone. "It's Terrell," she mouthed silently.

"Just hang up," I mouthed back. Ignoring me, she pushed the phone into my hand. I could have just as easily hung up myself, but apparently, doing so hadn't crossed my mind.

"Hello," I huffed, making my irritation clear in my tone.

"Your company gone yet?" he asked calmly.

"That ain't none of your business. Don't be calling here asking me questions!" I snapped.

"I'm not calling to argue with you, Ivy." Almost instantly I felt a sense of defeat. If I could get him to yell, scream, or say one foul thing, I would feel justified in hanging up on him.

"What are you calling for, Terrell?" I emerged from the closet and plopped down on my mattress set. Not wanting to waste any time, although I was quite tired, I started pulling more stuff out of a nearby box.

"I wanted to come by if your company was gone."

"You better not bring your ass around here!" I threatened, not intending to cuss. Goodness knows, after the revelation I'd received upon waking up this morning, I didn't need to cuss anybody out ever again. Terrell just seemed to frustrate me so bad.

"I just want to talk to you, Ivy. I know I messed up, but is all this really necessary?"

"Yes, it is," I said a little more calmly, crossing my arms over my chest, coaching myself to watch my mouth.

"Why?"

Why?? I couldn't believe he had the audacity to even let that question cross his lips. "Because I don't want to talk to you anymore, Terrell. I mean, I just don't see what we have to talk about. I've been begging you to talk to me for the past five years and you wouldn't talk to me then. Now I'm supposed to let you worry me to death repeating the same lies over and over again?"

"But, Ivy . . ."

"But nothing, Terrell. I really wish that you would stop calling me. We don't have anything else to talk about. Please."

"Well, can I at least speak to Terra?"

"She's busy and I'm hanging up now, Terrell. Don't call here no more, okay?" I could hear him still talking as I hung up the phone and dropped it beside me.

In my hand, I held Michael's and Michelle's high school diplomas. I really missed the twins but knew that their being away was what was best for their futures. I'd been prouder than a peacock the day they'd strutted across the stage at Hampton

High School during their high school graduation ceremony. Those two had me snapping pictures of nearly everyone in their entire graduating class as they said their final good-byes. Thinking of my own high school friends, it made me chuckle.

Chapter 12

All through intermediate school, Cindy and I were inseparable, but when we got to high school, we started to drift apart. I still loved her because we had been through so much together, but during our first year of high school, she had a baby boy and had to spend all her free time with him, which was totally understandable. I missed the closeness we'd shared a whole lot, and I still went to visit her often. Somehow, though, it just wasn't the same. . . .

I wasn't completely friendless in high school, though, because this was a time when I found out that it was so much easier to attract friends just by being myself and not trying so hard to impress people. Only thing is, that by this time, I realized what a real friend was and a lot of people just didn't meet the qualifications. Finally it wasn't so important to me whether I had a lot of friends or not.

There were five people whom I cared for a whole lot and with whom I started spending all my time. They didn't do a whole lot of talking behind my back, they listened when I needed to talk, and they made me laugh when I was down. It was a good thing that I started hanging out with these people around that particular time, because it just happened to be about the same time that Butch and I finally broke up and I really needed close friends to fill the void. My five friends and I did so much hanging out, talking and laughing when we were together or on the phone, that I didn't have much time to think about Butch.

Wayne was a no-nonsense person. He was the type who said what he meant and meant what he said. Even at that young age, when I didn't understand why it was good to be that way, I was so impressed by this quality of his. The thing about it was that although he was like that, he still was funny and made me laugh a lot.

He had five sisters. Two of them were close to his age, and three of them were much older. I think his parents passed away when he was young, so each of the older sisters raised one of the younger children. The sister Wayne lived with was named Betty, and she had a little girl named Joey.

I loved being with Wayne, and all through high school we were inseparable. When I dated a couple of other guys in high school, they never liked Wayne. I always had to make it clear to them that Wayne was my friend before I'd met them, and more than likely would still be after they'd left. They weren't too happy about it, but they knew there was nothing they could do but deal with it. We were just too close and everybody who knew us also knew what a special friendship we shared.

My second friend, Lydia, and I grew close during the first year of high school too, although this friendship was a little harder to get off the ground.

The reason behind this was that she and Cindy didn't care too much for each other and I felt like I was in the middle.

Lydia was the crazy one in the bunch. She could make us laugh just by the way she'd look at us sometimes. The thing about Lydia is not only how funny she was, but that she was equally as smart. Not just good grades either. Lydia was smart when it came to giving good advice about disagreements between boyfriends and girlfriends, family members, and friendships. When people came to her for advice (and lots of people did), she made sure that she heard both sides before voicing her opinion. When she did voice her opinion, she didn't care what anyone said or thought about it. She said what she wanted to say, and although sometimes what she said would hurt someone's feelings, the person couldn't hold it against her because what she said was always true.

Lydia was the first one in our group who had a driver's license, so she was the one who drove us in her family's car when we went to the high school football or basketball games. The thing about it was that she had to pick up her father from work at a certain time and she couldn't be late, so when she was taking us home from the games she'd start hollering, "Alright ya'll. Ya'll know I'm on the clock, so when I get to your corner, I ain't stopping! Just jump your ass out!" We'd all laugh, not taking her seriously. "Ya'll laughing; I'm serious," she'd say while holding her eyebrows up. Then sure enough when she got to our corner, she'd slow down, but she never came to a complete stop. "Git out! I ain't playing, git out!" Everybody in the car would crack up as we watched the one getting out literally jump from the moving vehicle. Once the rider was out and the door was shut, she'd speed off again with everybody else in the car dying laughing. The Bible says that "laughter does good like a medicine," and because of Lydia, I was "healed" lots of times. Even now I find myself laughing out loud.

My third friend, Lily, was actually a year behind us, so she didn't go to high school with us until the following year. Lily was a lot of fun too, although she'd get kind of quiet sometimes. She always seemed to have a lot on her mind. She was the popular type and was very involved in extracurricular activities. If she wasn't on the hockey team, she was playing the clarinet in the band. If she wasn't playing in the band, she was drum major of the band. If she wasn't the drum major, she was a cheerleader. I don't see how she kept up.

My best times with Lily were when we played jokes on people. We did stuff like fold a piece of paper, write someone's name on it, and drop it on the floor in the hallway. Most of the time it'd be a name of a popular person whom almost everybody in the school would recognize. Then we'd peek around the corner to see who would pick the paper up. When someone did pick it up and open it, it'd only say "NOSY ASS!" The person would look around to see if anybody was watching and then throw the note back down, while Lily and I, watching from a distance, would laugh.

Once I wrote her a letter and put my name and address in the middle of the envelope and Lily's name and address in the return address spot and mailed it to see if it would go through the postal system without the stamp. When we found out that it did, we started mailing each other letters all the time, although we saw each other at school, talked on the phone, or visited each other almost every day. After Mom found out what I was doing and told me that I could go to jail for doing something like that, I quickly stopped.

Lily was much shorter than I was, so she called me her "big sister", and although she was a year younger than I was, she was very wise in giving advice or offering her opinions. What I liked most is that she cared enough about me to also ask for mine.

Then there was Nick. Nick was a real sweetheart— the teddy bear type. Nick was the only one whom I felt comfortable enough around to actually cry on his shoulder. He played on the football team, so he couldn't be with us at the games, but we hung out a lot together at school, especially at lunchtime. He also played the trumpet in the school band, and he played so well that he often had a solo whenever the band did a concert.

I remember once when he came over to my house and my little niece answered the door. When he told her that his name was Nick, she hollered that "Dick" was at the door. (Little kids can be so embarrassing to teenagers sometimes.)

I remember another time Nick took me to a concert to see the group War. Cindy braided my hair real pretty. It all went to one side and ended with a giant Afro puff. I had on this two-piece Hawaiian print halter set that Cindy let me borrow. She also loaned me some flower earrings just like the flowers on the halter set. I just *knew* I was looking good! Overall, I was bored at the concert, though, because

War was one of those groups that sung one song for about a half an hour, and almost everybody in the whole coliseum was either already high or getting high right then. Between the loud music and the smell of marijuana, I got a terrible headache and was ready to go home.

When Nick slowly broke away from us because he started dating someone who had already graduated the previous year, I was so jealous. I guess it was because I knew that Nick would have made the perfect boyfriend and I didn't take advantage of the opportunity that I had had to make him mine. He and his girlfriend had a precious baby boy who had thick eyebrows exactly like Nick's.

Last but not least, there was Cookie. Cookie was not as loud or crazy as the rest of us because she was the most sensitive one in the group. Cookie, like Wayne, lost her parents when she was young and was being raised by her grandmother. In the seventies, you could kind of tell which kids were being raised by their grandmother because they were always "different." Somehow they just didn't seem to raise as much hell as everybody else. We talked about Cookie and called her "soft," because at that time we thought there was something wrong with being that way. The thing about it was, I was exactly the same way but too weak to show it. Cookie hung right in there with us, though, laughing at how we messed with other people. Cookie dated a senior, so she didn't spend a lot of time with us when we weren't at school.

Wayne, Lydia, Nick, Lily, Cookie, and I were inseparable in school. There were a few others, but these were my very best friends. During our senior year, we were together so much that it may have looked like we didn't have time for anybody else, but we did, because all of us dated people who were not in the group. Sometimes they were jealous of the time we spent with our "special group," but we didn't care. We thought that nothing could keep us apart, but after high school, we all went our separate ways.

It was really a good thing that I was at a point in my memories that was happy, because beside my bed, a stack of bills caught my eye. I was wondering how I would financially manage without Terrell. I was already working at night and going to school during the day. As I thought about it more, though, I realized that with the way Terrell had been wasting his money on drugs and liquor, I actually had been managing financially all along.

It took my blood, sweat, and tears to get this apartment, and there was no way I could let Terrell come in and snatch the rug out from me again. Standing there explaining to the twenty-something-year-old leasing consultant why I had more unpaid debts than I was ready to admit to had been humiliating.

"Miss, I have to put a roof over my baby's head. Like I said, most of these debts were made by my husband, and we aren't together anymore."

"I understand that, ma'am. However, there are specific guidelines that come through our home office that we are supposed to use to qualify our tenants. With some of these things that are showing up on your credit report, it just reflects that you would be considered a high risk."

This girl who had been sitting there telling me I

was a high risk probably lived at home with her parents not paying a dime of rent to anybody or knowing the first thing about life. *Stay humble Ivy, stay humble,* I had thought.

"I understand what you are saying, and that there are guidelines, but none of those creditors are landlords," I had said in my defense. "I've always paid my rent, miss, and I am just asking that some consideration be given to my extenuating circumstances." While I'd pleaded with her with my mouth, in my head I was pleading with God. I couldn't think of any other words besides *Please, Lord Jesus, please!* I wonder if God was in heaven with that little red blouse hanging off the hook of His fingers contemplating a decision. Well, needless to say, His mercy and grace endured, because after letting me panic for nearly a week, the same young lady called me a few days ago to let me know my application had miraculously been approved.

Chapter 13

I didn't go to college right away, because, well, the truth is, I don't know why. I guess I didn't have a reason. The following year, when I did decide to go, I was discouraged because the first college I applied to, which happened to be a very prestigious and privately owned school, denied my application because my high school grades weren't good enough. I was crushed. When I applied to a couple of other state-owned colleges, they accepted me. I decided on an in-state, predominantly black college, Virginia State.

I could barely sleep the night before I left for Virginia State wondering what kind of person my roommate would be. What would she look like? Would she be a party animal or a bookworm? Would she be boy crazy or a square?

Before I got to the room good, I heard Stevie Wonder loudly singing "Knocks Me Off My Feet." *Okay, at least we like the same kind of music,* I thought.

Bonnie was from Philly, and she looked just like her name. She was petite, had flawless dark skin, the cutest dimpled smile you ever wanted to see, and short, thick hair.

As soon as I got unpacked, I went walking around the campus. I started wishing that I had come the year before, because by the way things looked, I knew that I was going to like it. There were people hanging out and loud music coming from dorm windows and cars everywhere. You could easily tell the freshmen who were just getting there, because they would walk around in groups trying not to look so lost.

The students who had been there previously were much more confident. If they walked in groups, it was with their fraternity brothers or sorority sisters as they proudly wore their colors and did their calls. If they walked alone, it wasn't for long, because they soon would see someone else who had previously been there and they would run up to each other with squeals, hugs, or dap.

Although Bonnie and I had a different group of friends, her friends were cool. Once when all of her friends came down to our room, one of them looked at me and yelled with excitement, "I know you!" It was actually Gloria. I had no clue as to who she was, but it was obvious that she knew me from high school because she named everybody I used to hang out with: Wayne, Nick, Lydia, Lily, and Cookie. I think that because of the closeness of our "group," a whole lot more people knew us than we knew them.

The next time I saw Gloria, she was walking with someone whom I knew I recognized. I just couldn't quite remember from where. When I took a closer look, there was no mistaking who she was.

"*Nicky?*"

"Ivy?"

It was Nicky, my friend who lived across the street from me when I first moved to Virginia from Cleveland! Only by then, she went by her more sophisticated, real name of Tiajuana. We must've hugged and screamed in each other's ear for at least a full minute. Everything about her was the same, including her attire. The girl dressed to kill.

My attitude was totally opposite what it was in high school. I was now wondering what I wanted to do other than just go to class. I thought about trying out for the marching band, joining the gospel choir, auditioning for the plays, pledging a sorority, or being a fraternity sweetheart. There was so much going on.

When I went to gym class and the girl's basketball team coach saw me, she immediately started in on me just like my high school's team coach did.

"Have you ever played ball?" she asked.

"No," I answered.

"You really should," she persisted.

"I don't know. . . ."

"Why not?"

"Because I never played before and I've seen those girls play. They're good, and I don't want to make a fool out of myself out there trying to play with them."

"But with practice, you could be good just like them. Don't worry about it; we'll work with you. Just start coming to practice and if you don't feel comfortable enough to jump in right away, just sit the first couple of practices out. Start when *you* feel comfortable enough. We still have time. The season doesn't start for another few months."

I started to consider it, but the deciding factor was the stigma that was attached to the girl's basketball team. A lot of them were gay and had no problem letting people know it. On top of that, it seemed that they were strongly influential.

I say this because I particularly remember a girl who was a majorette. This was a very pretty girl, but she had a certain sadness in her eyes. I've always heard that you can tell a lot about a person by looking in his or her eyes and that the eyes are "the windows of the soul." I wondered if the sadness I saw in the girl's eyes was a sign of weakness or vulnerability because this girl didn't seem to have gay qualities at first. I'd personally seen her with a few guys and she seemed to enjoy their company as they did hers. Keep in mind, this was a majorette and their uniforms were real skimpy, so they had no problem attracting the attention of any guy on campus unless the guy was already committed to someone else. Really committed. Anyway, the next thing I knew, this majorette had "hooked up" with one of the girl basketball players who was also a Muslim, and the majorette stopped associating with everybody, male and female, except of course the girl basketball players. She was still a majorette, and an awesome one at that. She could twirl the baton like nobody's business, and all the majorettes smiled when they performed so she did too, but at the same time, she still had that sad look in her eyes. The only time students ever saw her was when the band practiced or performed, or when somebody shared a class with her. Soon rumors started spreading that she and the girl basketball player had gotten "married," and sure enough, both of them had started wearing a small band on their left ring finger. Years later, I saw the same girl on a Greyhound bus. She had on Muslim clothing with everything covered except her eyes, but I knew it was her—I'll never forget those eyes.

I'm not judging gays or Muslims. I've always felt that everyone's lifestyle or religion is his or her own business. I just felt that in college your reputation meant a lot, and I didn't want anyone on the basketball team thinking that they could influence me to be gay, or anyone who wasn't on the team thinking I was already that way. I asked a couple of my "newfound" friends what they thought. They unanimously agreed and I decided not to play. Although to this day I still don't regret joining the team, that decision was the first of many mistakes that I made in life by letting others make *my* final decisions. . . .

All the extra things that I wanted to do quickly washed down the drain because I found out that to do any of these things took a lot of practice, determination, or kissing up. The first two of these things I still had not developed the drive to do. The latter I simply refused to.

I finally got tired of wearing my Afro and decided to get my first perm. (I thought about Tawanna Monk back in Cleveland, who was getting them at least eleven years before, and wondered what her hair looked like about this time.) One of my friends named Pam referred me to her beautician.

"She's an older lady, Ivy, and her shop is not all fabulous, but she knows what she's doing." That's all I needed to hear. Besides, I believed Pam because she kept her hair looking good. Most of the time, she wore it back with a headband and curled slightly under, and it was always bone straight with a lot of body.

Pam was right about the shop not being fabulous. It was dark and dusty, and the stations were so close together you almost had to do the Electric Slide to get around in there, but after the lady got finished, my hair was gorgeous. I had worn my hair in an Afro for so long that I hadn't realized how long it had grown. I now wore it in a ponytail and it was too cute (or at least I thought so, which was most important).

In every girl's clique at Virginia State, there was one person who stood out. People really loved this person because in spite of her shortcomings, she was fun to be around. This person was up on the campus gossip, because she knew some of everybody. She had nice clothes that she never minded sharing (unless they were brand new, of course), and whatever mood she was in for the day was so strong that everybody in the group felt it. Although her room was junky, she knew exactly where everything was, down to the smallest earring back. Anybody was welcome to anything unless there was a note attached to it in some way stating otherwise. Her room was chosen as the "hangout" room, and people went there to find something to eat or even catch a nap, as though they had no room of their own. In our clique, this person was Patrice.

Patrice was a trip. Whenever we had time, we would listen to music in her room and show each other the latest dance steps. We got everything down to a tee except the hustle. We couldn't understand why nobody could get it right, because at the dances we could hustle all night. What we didn't understand was that the hustle was a dance that you couldn't teach or practice. It was one of those dances that you just did on the spot while following the guy's lead.

Another thing I remember we did in Patrice's room, which was so much fun, was to have talent shows. It was so funny because everybody would be trying to sing whatever the latest song was, like "The Beat Goes On," "The Closer I Get to You," "Ain't No Stopping Us Now," or "After the Love Has Gone." When it was Patrice's turn, she'd get up there, announce that she wanted to sing a song from her church choir, and bust out and start singing "We Come This Far by Faith." Then I wouldn't have any more sense than to join in with her, and we'd be harmonizing away. We could never get through the whole song, though, for laughing at our own selves.

Although all of us in the group had our own beliefs, habits, likes, and dislikes, we still had a great amount of influence on each other. One of the girls in the group, who was from New Jersey, Felicia, was a vegetarian. I asked her a lot of questions about it and she told me a lot of different reasons why meat was bad for us. Almost immediately, I became a vegetarian too.

Another time someone named Medina invited me to one of her Jehovah's Witness Bible study meetings. I was going, but I made the mistake of mentioning it to Mom. I tried to convince her that I wasn't considering conversion and was just going

out of curiosity, but she still almost had a connip-
tion, so I didn't go.

Our little clique did everything together except
go to class, because we had different majors. After
our morning classes, we all would meet in Patrice's
room before going to lunch. Then we'd separate
again for our afternoon classes. On days when we
didn't have afternoon classes, we'd go to Patrice's
or our own room for a nap.

I never had afternoon classes because I was a
morning person and would always schedule my
classes back-to-back from 8:00 A.M. to 1:00 P.M. I
think the reason I never had a problem getting up
was that I went to sleep so early. I got on everybody's nerves the way I slept all the time, because
they said I was missing out on everything, like the
card games, when someone down the hall started
arguing, when they peeked out in the halls to see
what guy was sneaking to or from what girl's room,
or the late-night walks to the store to get something
to snack on. Eventually they got used to it, though,
because they saw that all of their fussing didn't
change me.

"If Ivy ever lay across your bed close to nighttime,
don't even bother trying to wake her up. Just pull
her shoes off and roll her over—she's there for the
night," Gloria used to say.

Gloria was another trip. I remember once when I
was in the library and she came in. I was supposed
to have been working on some kind of paper but
got frustrated because I couldn't find any good resources, so I purposefully started putting the drawers of the card catalog back in the wrong places.

When Gloria figured out what I was doing, she looked at me with a slight frown.

"That's not where that goes," she said.

"I know," I said, looking down at her with a devious smile. She thought it was funny and immediately started doing it too. It was a wonder that we didn't get caught. After we thought we had the drawers mixed up enough, we both left the library cracking up.

Pam and I were the only two out of the group who got up early enough for breakfast. When she didn't go, I had to go alone. I hated that, because I didn't have anybody with me to help me talk about people . . . behind their backs of course.

Chapter 14

I placed Michael's and Michelle's high school memorabilia on the wall in the hallway, along with their senior portraits, and smiled. As I stared at Michael's photo, I subconsciously began to frown. Now that he was a full-grown man, he looked so much like his daddy, whom I happened to be mad at, although I thought our love would last forever.

I'd met James during my second year in college. I was *too* upset because I was the only one in our "group" who had been assigned to a different dorm. I tried to look at the bright side, which was that the dorm where I was assigned was the only dorm on campus where each room had a private bathroom. Still, I couldn't be convinced that this was better than being away from the rest of my friends.

I was continually in Patrice's room that year, because I had a weirdo for a roommate and I couldn't stand her. When I say that, I don't mean we couldn't get along, because we never said an unkind word to each other, but she was just so strange that she was uncomfortable to be around. She was as smart as a whip (I'm assuming so because she was a math major and kept a high GPA), but she did all kinds of stupid stuff like wear sunglasses in the room because the light was too bright instead of just turning the light off. She also used to talk to herself a lot. Her boyfriend was just as strange as she was. He came to our room all times of the day or night so they could get high, get their "groove on," or both. I always put my head under my covers and tried to muffle the sounds they made. I hated it most when he came in the mornings and they went in the bathroom together for a morning "quickie," because it made me late for class. Talk about inconsideration.

The same year that I was roommates with the weirdo, Patrice and her boyfriend, Rueben, introduced me to James Williams. James and Rueben both attended William & Mary, a predominantly white, hard-to-get-into school. The meeting was prearranged by me and Patrice, so when Rueben and James got to Patrice's dorm, I was already nervously waiting in her room.

I was instantly impressed with James. He was tall, had a really nice build, and although his head was a little bigger than I preferred, he had big brown eyes to match and the brightest smile that I've ever seen on a man. After James and I met, we decided to go back to my room and talk. Luckily, the weirdo wasn't there. We made plans for me to visit him at his college the next weekend.

James's school was the most beautiful college I ever saw. It was wintertime, and at my school, the snow had mixed with dirt, making ugly mounds all over campus. At W&M, however, it looked like Winter

Wonderland. I couldn't stop staring out of James's dorm room window.

There was a lake in the center of the campus that separated the girls' dorms from the boys' dorms. There was a bridge that crossed the lake, and in the middle of the bridge, there was a big gazebo. The lake was frozen and people were actually ice skating on it. As he told me of the time he got up enough courage to walk across the frozen lake, James laughed and demonstrated how he tested the thickness of the ice with each step. He said in the spring and summer the students fished and had canoe races in the lake too.

Then he took me on a tour of the campus. The cafeteria looked like a restaurant, and the food was laid out buffet style and not slammed on the plates by mean women wearing hairnets, like at Virginia State. The gym looked like a coliseum on the inside, and the student union was a beautiful building with a spiral staircase in the middle of it. The front of the student union was made of glass and faced the lake.

While we were in the student union, a dog with dark, weird-looking eyes came up to James and slowly wagged his tail. James started to smile and pet the dog. When he saw the questioned look on my face, he explained that the dog was called "Space Dog" because one of the kids at the college had supposedly given him some drugs and it "messed the dog up." He continued to explain that the dog rarely ever paid anybody too much attention, so when he did, quite naturally that person felt special. Most of the time, though, the dog just walked around slowly like he was spaced out.

James and Rueben had football scholarships.

Patrice and I looked forward to the weekends so that we could go to their football games instead of our own, because the only reason we really went to our own games anyway was to see the cheerleaders and the band. There were so many people at the William & Mary games that in my mind they could have been mistaken for professional NFL games. I felt so special when I went to the "Will Call" window and picked up the ticket James had waiting for me.

One thing Virginia State did have on William & Mary was the band; its band wasn't half as good as ours. Its cheerleaders weren't that good either, because all they did was spell a whole lot of words through megaphones and stand on each other's shoulders. On the other hand, our band was something else. It always played the latest songs while we jammed in the stands. Our cheerleaders were outstanding too, doing amazing stunts and awesome dance routines to the band's music.

The most exciting game I went to was when the game announcer stated that Virginia State had reached university status. Everybody went off. The band members played every song they had ever practiced and even a few that they hadn't, and the cheerleaders started flipping and flying all over the place, as we hollered and jammed to the music. We actually had a party in the stands. We forgot all about the poor football players on the field struggling to win the game. It didn't even matter to us anymore. Virginia State College had finally become Virginia State University!

Nevertheless, Patrice and I didn't mind sacrificing all of this good entertainment to see our boyfriends play ball and spend time with them afterward. Before

I realized it, I was spending more time at James's college than I was at my own. Even when his team went out of town to play, I still went there and waited in his room for him to come back.

Slowly, my taste in music began to change. I still loved the black music artists, but I found myself listening more to songs by Phil Collins, Christopher Cross, Kenny Loggins, and The Doobie Brothers. My favorite was "What You Won't Do for Love" by Bobby Caldwell, and I purely fell in love with Michael McDonald of the Doobies, especially when he broke away from the group and went solo. The man was awesome, and right up to this day, he's one of my favorites.

Eventually, James noticed the time I was spending there. Although he enjoyed my company, he was concerned because the weekends started spilling over into the weekdays and he knew I couldn't have possibly been studying like I should have been.

"Ivy, please get your education, because I'm going to get mine," he once said.

"Don't worry, I'm okay," I answered.

The truth was that I really wasn't. My major was supposed to be special education, but I changed it to James, sleeping, and the card game, Spades.

Chapter 15

James was also in the army ROTC program. One summer he went away for training. I missed him so much. Before he went away, I promised I would write him every day. Lots of people say this when most of the time they just mean that they're going to write a lot. Then some people write letters every day but don't actually mail them. I literally wrote and mailed James a letter *every day*.

Before I knew it the summer had passed, and the fall semester had begun.

James had pledged the fraternity the previous year. His line name was "Headquarters," because of his big head. I was shocked to find out he was pledging, because it was while I was visiting him, and pledgees were not allowed to spend time with their girlfriends at the college I attended.

On this particular weekend, there was a knock on his door.

"I'm not going," James said and then closed the door.

It was then when I found out that James was "on line."

"How can you tell them what you ain't gone do while you're pledging?" I asked him.

"Why not?" he answered. Evidently, James hadn't heard about what pledging was like on a black school's campus. When I told him of things that I had heard and actually witnessed, he didn't believe me.

"That's crazy. No one could actually lose their self-respect like that to be a part of something," he said while shaking his head. A few weeks later the pledging line James was on visited another black college and he witnessed the hazing for himself.

"I couldn't believe it, Ivy. Ain't no way I would've pledged if I had to go through the things I saw."

The saddest thing that happened while I was at Virginia State was when two people died while pledging. I had just come back from visiting James, and right away, I noticed that the aura on campus was very strange. No one was in sight, everything was strangely quiet, and floodlights kept going across the sky. Because it was so late, I just went to bed. I didn't find out what had actually happened until the next day when I was in history class and the professor was talking about it.

You see, our college campus was built over a river. Sometimes during the day, we followed a certain path through a wooded area down to the river where the waters rushed over rocks. It was a nice place to play, romance, study, or just be alone. Once I even had some pictures of myself made down there. At night, though, this was a totally different place because all you saw was the dark woods and all you heard was the loud rushing water, and it was really spooky.

Anyway, this particular fraternity and its sister sorority supposedly took their pledge lines down to the river to "baptize" them on the night they were "going over." While they were being baptized, strong water currents carried one of the boys and one of the girls away. They had been missing for almost a week before the truth finally came out. The river was dragged until the bodies of the boy and girl were found.

About the time that this happened, it was my and James third year together, and I was spending every weekend with him. We didn't even plan it anymore. It was just automatically understood that I would be with him. Once when I was in his dorm room sitting at his desk, I saw the name "Michael Ray Williams" written on his desk pad.

"Who's that?" I asked him.

"That's what I want to name my son whenever I have one," he answered.

"Oh," I said.

Just like the previous year, James was concerned about my study time. I managed to convince him that I was okay until eventually he stopped asking. The truth was that at the end of that semester I was placed on academic probation. . . .

That fall, I was roommates with Patrice. We lived in the newest dorm on campus, which had just been finished that summer and was a coed dorm. We started the routine all over again of going to the games at James and Rueben's school, and seldom going to our own.

Patrice was still head of our campus clique, and although some of the members had changed, it was basically the same. Because we were actually roommates, though, I really got a chance to know Patrice by the long, in-depth conversations that we had. We spent hours on end sharing the histories of our past and plans for our futures. Together, we cried and laughed a lot. Especially laughed. That girl ain't have good sense. One thing I knew for sure, she really loved her boyfriend, Rueben. She talked about that man *all* the time. He was her high school sweetheart and I'm pretty sure that they had problems just like everybody else (as a matter of fact, I'm *really* sure that they did, because I'm the one who had to sit up half the night and listen to them!), but of all the couples who were together in high school and college, Rueben and Patrice are the only ones I know of who got married soon after graduation and are still together to this day.

That same semester, I scheduled all my classes in the evening so that I could work during the day. I got a job at Hardee's. It seemed like a good idea at first, but lots of times when I worked in the day and went to class in the evening, I came home from class and fell asleep instead of studying. Other times I just slept through the time that I was supposed to be in class. I eventually just dropped out of school, thinking that it was no big deal—I would come back the following semester. Little did I know that the "following semester" wouldn't come until twenty-one years later.

That May, James received his bachelor of arts degree.

Chapter 16

After I dropped out of school, I got closer to God. A lot of people say that they "get more into the church," but trust me, there is a difference. I'm more than sure you know that everyone in the "church" is not close to God. Anyway, I read the Bible every day and prayed for some kind of direction in my life. My favorite person in the Old Testament to read about was (and still is) David, because he was always doing something he had no business doing yet he loved the Lord. Regardless of the trouble he seemed to get himself into, God knew how much David loved Him and because David had no problem admitting he was wrong and begging God for forgiveness, He delivered David each time. In the book of Psalms, I really loved to read Psalm 34, which was written by David. Especially verse 22, which says, "The Lord redeemeth the souls of His servants, and none of them that trust in Him shall be desolate." I wrote it on an index card and taped it to the headboard of my bed so that it would be the last thing I read at night and the first thing I read each morning. Just like David, I loved the Lord, but somehow always missed the mark. . . .

"I'm pregnant."

"How do you know? It's not your time yet."

"I just know. A voice told me."

James started to laugh. "A voice, huh? Why don't you ask the voice for some numbers to play?" he joked.

"Okay, keep laughing. You'll see," I said. I waited a few weeks later before I went to the clinic to have a test. It came back positive.

We both had mixed feelings about it, because I was really looking forward to going back to school, and James was looking forward to getting a job in the field of his degree, but all of that quickly changed.

James was obligated to the army to either be in the reserves or go active duty because he had received funds from the army while he was in the college ROTC program. He was currently in the reserves, but he wanted security benefits for the baby and me as soon as possible, so he changed his plans and went on active duty.

We were married that August. I didn't have a big wedding party, because I wasn't working with a whole lot of money. Of course, Patrice was my maid of honor, and my cousin Edith's two children, Dina and Deon, were the flower girl and ring bearer. That was it. Although I didn't have a lot of decorations, it seemed like a lot because I set them up alone. I was still in the church hanging flowers on the rented arch about an hour before the wedding was due to begin. Besides the arch, I only had the aisle roll. I can't even remember if I had the unity candle. Although several church members who were still there from the morning service asked me what was I doing there and why wasn't I at home getting ready, they didn't offer to help.

Medina came to my house to help me get ready. She saved the day by making me laugh when she had to threaten to kill me if I didn't let her make my face up. I never liked wearing make-up, but she swore by it. Aunt May styled my hair in beautiful curls, but by the time the wedding was about to start, I had sweated all the curls out, so I wore my hair all pulled back. My mother made my dress and I borrowed a headpiece. I wasn't completely satisfied, but considering the circumstances, I suppose I looked okay. Medina chauffeured me in my little white car to the church.

My brother escorted me down the aisle and gave me away in lieu of my father, whom I hadn't seen in years, to James, who looked so handsome (although a bit nervous) in his army dress greens.

During the wedding, Liz sang one of my church favorites, "Ordinary People." Although it wasn't a wedding song, I chose it because I loved to hear her sing it and it was supposed to be *my* day. I tried hard to concentrate on the moment and stop wondering so much as Bishop Edison held my wedding band up and explained that just like it continued in a circle and had no end, the love that James and I had for each other was supposed to be never ending. . . .

My Uncle Ed was a member of this social club where we had the reception. When we got there, the food was still all covered up on the tables where we had left it before the wedding. I was all to pieces.

Now that I think about it, I don't think anybody helped because I didn't ask specific people to do specific things. Maybe they thought I already had the help I needed; I don't know. Nevertheless, after we got it together it turned out pretty nice.

Of course Lydia was there keeping me laughing with her crazy self, along with some people from college whom I didn't even expect to come. Even Aunt Mary was there from Cleveland.

James and I danced the first dance to Peabo Bryson's "Hold on to the World." It was a long day and I was glad when it was over. Little did I know, "it" had only just begun. . . .

While James waited for his military orders, we lived with his aunt. She was happy to have us there and very determined not to get in our business when we had disagreements.

I continued to visit my doctor as scheduled. Although I still had my little car, lots of times I walked for the exercise.

"Your iron is very low. What are you eating?" the doctor once asked me.

"I'm a vegetarian," I answered, with a smile, thinking that it would impress the doctor. I had picked that up in college.

"Well, maybe you should put that off for a while, because you really need the iron in meat for the baby."

Around my fourth or fifth month, the doctor was concerned about the weight I was gaining.

"I knew I would gain a lot when I started to eat meat again," I started to whine.

"That's not it. You shouldn't be gaining this fast. I'm going to send you to the hospital for an ultrasound. Come back here right after you leave there," he said as he scribbled something on paper. When I went back to the doctor's office the next day, he kept laughing at me.

"What's so funny?" I continued to ask.

"You're having twins," he said, then laughed. Because he kept laughing, I thought he was playing. I went to the waiting room and got James, who happened to be with me that day. When we stood before the doctor together, I asked him to repeat what he had said to James.

"Your wife is having twins." That time he didn't crack a smile. James smiled all the way home, assuring me that everything would be okay. I had just finished crocheting a baby blanket that morning. When I got home, I started on another one. . . .

Later, we got our first apartment right down the street from James's father and stepmom. While James continued to wait for his orders, he got a job at 7-Eleven. Lydia and her younger sister kept me going. We usually went to the mall or to different places to eat. They kept me laughing, with their crazy selves. While James was at work in the evening, they stayed over at our house to keep me company.

Medina was still keeping in touch with me by mail. Our letters from each other had grown to a large number by then, because a whole year had passed since I'd first dropped out of school and we'd first started to write to each other.

Gloria also visited me a lot, but she and Lydia didn't care that much for each other and it made me so uncomfortable. (All through school, college, and my adult years, I had friends who "tolerated" each other for my sake. Mom said my friends were like bicycle tire spokes and I was like the hub that held them all together.)

The year was 1982 and I was almost twenty-four years old. The doctor had warned me to stop eating so much sugar and salt, but I didn't listen. (Very recently, I learned that the way I had been eating hadn't been the cause of the serious case of toxemia that I had developed. Even if it hadn't caused it directly, though, I'm sure it had had something to do with it, because my blood pressure had been so high.) My feet and hands started to swell and the doctor told me to stay off my feet as much as possible.

I asked James to bring me a soda and a bag of chips home every night and he did. He knew that I wasn't supposed to have it, but I think he did it anyway to keep me from getting so upset.

One particular night when he came in and gave me my midnight snack and went down the hall to bed, he said he heard some thumping in the living room, which is where I was. He said that when he came back up there, I was in the middle of the floor having convulsions. His first reaction was to put his finger in my mouth to keep me from swallowing my tongue. I think he still has a mark on his hand today to show from it. We didn't have a phone, so James banged on the neighbor's door to call an ambulance. James said that on the way to the hospital between the convulsions, I was hallucinating and calling for my daddy.

I couldn't (and still can't) remember what happened, but when I got to the hospital, right before I went into the operating room, I remember hearing my mom's voice. "Remember your verse," it said. From that point on, all I know is what James and my other family members told me. . . .

Someone told me that I almost died. Someone told me that although Bishop Edison's daughter had a baby on the very same day I did, he still came to see me and pray for me. Someone told me that I almost died. Someone told me that it was decided who would take care of the babies. Someone told me that I almost died. Someone told me that I looked like a monster. Someone told me that I almost died. Someone told me that James never left my side. Someone told me that I almost died. Someone told me that my doctor said he could save either me or the twins, but not all three of us. Someone told me that I almost died. Someone told me that almost a week had passed since I had the C-section, but still James refused to see the babies, because he was determined that we were going to see them *together*. Someone told me that I almost died. . . .

I came around a week later. The first thing I saw was people who seemed to be floating around dressed in white. I thought I had died and was in Heaven. I always joke a lot and people think that I'm joking whenever I say this, but I'm not. I'm serious. I closed my eyes and smiled. When I opened them again, I saw James standing there in a blue jacket. I was disappointed that I wasn't in Heaven, but I was glad to see the smile on James's face. I put my hand on my stomach and felt the flatness.

"The babies," I whispered.

Although I didn't think that it could, James's smile got even wider. He held up one finger.

"We have one boy and one girl," he said.

I could tell the personality difference in the twins when the nurse first brought them to us. For some reason, she brought them in one at a time.

The little boy was first. He had on a tiny blue hat. His face was so tiny that if I made a circle with the tip of my middle finger touching the tip of my thumb, I could frame his eyes, nose, and mouth with it. He wasn't asleep, but for some reason, he wouldn't open his eyes. Maybe it was because I wasn't prepared for it, but when he finally did and his little glassy eyes looked right into mine, my heart almost melted. He was so precious. He didn't even move. He just lay there and stared at me until the nurse brought in our little girl and I passed our little boy to James.

Then the nurse handed the little girl to me. She had on a pink cap. It was pulled down right to her eyes and turned sideways as if it was that way because of her moving her head around in it so much. Her eyes were wide open as she peeked from under the hat to see what was going on around her. She never kept still, but wiggled around as she waved her little fist in the air and cried. *Oh . . . oh*, I thought. I still held her close and kissed her, even though she let me know that she didn't like it.

They were seven weeks premature. He weighed five pounds and ten ounces. She weighed five pounds and two ounces. I thought about the name written on James's desk pad in his college dorm room at William & Mary. We named the twins Michael Ray and Michelle Renee.

As promised, I called Medina to let her know I had had the twins. She couldn't believe it.

"No you didn't, Ivy. Stop lying; you ain't have nothing," she kept repeating. She said that although she knew I was pregnant with the twins and we had kept in close contact the whole time I carried them, to her it was just unbelievable. I knew what she meant, because I could hardly believe it myself. . . .

Chapter 17

Soon after I had the twins, James got orders to leave the state. Although I missed him a lot, I still had plenty of help with the twins from his and my family. It seemed like everybody was anxious to keep them.

Gloria was working in the mall at the portrait studio, which just happened to be in the baby department of the store, so she was forever picking up something "cute" for them as well as begging me to have more pictures made every other month. She bought them their christening outfits—Michael, a little white tuxedo, and Michelle, a long white dress with a bonnet. The little outfits were so precious. Lydia was chosen to be their godmother and my Uncle Ed, their godfather.

Lydia stayed at the apartment with me to help out. I really don't know what I would've done without her. Whenever we took the twins out, we dressed them just alike taking special care to stay away from the traditional pink and blue. It was so funny when people asked us if they were identical because when we said no, some argued that they were because they "looked just alike." (At that time, the only reason I knew that the twins weren't identical was that the doctor had told me they weren't. It wasn't until many years later that I learned that identical twins are actually the result of one seed being split in half after being fertilized and fraternal twins are the result of two separate seeds being fertilized at the same time. That's why identical twins are always the same sex and look exactly alike—they are from the same seed. That information never ceased to amaze me and make me think of how awesome God is.)

Besides taking care of the twins, we used to sit around and talk about school days and listen to music a lot. Luther Vandross had just come out with his first album. We loved "A House Is Not a Home" to death and sung along with Luther from the bottom of our hearts whenever we played it.

When James came back, he had orders to go to Germany. I didn't want to go. James was hurt that I felt that way, but he just ignored my complaints and continuously tried to encourage me.

"You'll be all right," he kept telling me. He said I had to leave my car in the States. I can't remember if he said he thought it was, or the military would think it was, too old to be shipped. Nevertheless, I wasn't too happy about it, because it was my first little car that I had worked so hard for, but I didn't have a choice. Besides, he had just bought a brand new car that he didn't mind me driving. It was a sporty red Dodge Omni. I gave my car to my mom. I may not have been too happy, but Mom sure was.

Time moved fast, and before we knew it, it was time

to leave. My immediate family met for dinner and then we went to Olan Mills to take a family portrait before I left. Of everybody in the picture, I had the weakest smile. Later, Lydia, Lily, Gloria, and I had a going away get-together. We went to Pizza Hut. We had a ball; we laughed a lot, but it only made it harder for me to leave. . . .

That March I turned twenty-four, the twins were about six months, and I was feeling good, because I had worked so hard to lose weight and everyone I met told me that I didn't look twenty-four, much less like I had just given birth to twins. Then it was about the end of July, I think, but I do remember it being hot that day. Real hot. I was so uncomfortable, but not only from the heat. The day had finally come for us to leave for Germany. . . .

Mom said it did something to her to see us walking down the hall together in the airport—me and James, each holding a baby. She just stood there and watched as we walked farther and farther away. . . .

It was my first time ever on an airplane. It was the biggest plane I'd ever seen in my life. I guess that sounds contradictory, but I had seen the inside of planes on television and in movies and none of them seemed as big as this one. There were three columns that were eight seats wide, so that meant each row had twenty-four seats. I don't know how many rows there were, but from the front of the plane, they looked endless. I made sure that I sat by the window so that I could get the full effect of my first plane ride.

The attendants were very nice at making sure we

had everything we needed. When we took off, it felt like my very heart was trying to come through my back. I looked out the window as everything on the ground started to get smaller and smaller. Then the ground actually started to look like a map in green, brown, and blue. While looking down at the earth, I again thought about how awesome God was, for He had made it with His own hands. As fast as an airplane travels, I thought that I would feel that pulling sensation the whole way, but after we were in the air, it was as if I were sitting in a house or something. I was truly amazed.

Soon the excitement died down and the babies fell asleep. So did I. James woke me when they brought out dinner, then they showed a movie. I tried to watch it but all I could think of was my family and friends I was leaving and the foreign country I was going to. I went to sleep again. It seemed to be the only way I could forget about everything. . . .

The most amazing thing about the trip was when everybody was getting ready to go to sleep for the night. I looked at my watch and it was about 12:00 midnight. When I looked out the window, though, it was broad daylight. The pilot announced that the correct time was 8:00 A.M. We were actually crossing the time zone that I had heard so much about.

A shade came across the window to make the plane dark. I had slept so long that I felt I had already slept for the night, so, as everybody else slept, I just lay there and thought about my life I was leaving the United States: Mom, Dad, Jr., Liz, Clarita, my high school friends, my college friends, my children. *Wow, my children. I actually have two children,* I thought. And

James. I looked over at him. I thought he was asleep but he was looking right back at me. He seemed to have been reading my mind.

"You'll be all right," he whispered.

The funniest part of the whole trip was the flight attendants. They were the very same ladies on the plane as when we started out (I mean, I don't remember us stopping in midair and picking up anybody else), but now they were speaking with English accents. I wondered if that was part of their training.

Because James was in ROTC in college, he was a commissioned officer and his rank was second lieutenant. He was treated with the utmost respect from the time we hit Germany. Other officers were there to meet us. As James shook hands with them and they introduced themselves, my eyes roamed the airport, which was amazingly large. There were thousands of people rushing back and forth, and all different kinds of crowded shops and eating places as far as my eyes could see. Of course I had seen moving stairs before, but this was the first time I saw floors actually move. When I finally gave my sense of sight a break, my sense of hearing instantly kicked in. That's when it hit me that we were *really* in a foreign country, because as far as my ears could hear, we were the only ones speaking English.

Then came the ride to the base where James was stationed. It was so long. I noticed something strange about the ride but couldn't figure it out. James saw the look on my face and laughed.

"You notice anything strange?" he asked me. He was so focused on my every thought and move, because he knew how much I didn't want to be there, and he continually tried to comfort me.

"Yeah, but I can't figure it out," I said. Because he saw a smile on my face, he knew that I wasn't exactly frustrated, just puzzled. He let me think about it a few more minutes before he told me that everyone was driving on the left side of the street, instead of the right side, like we did at home. Also, there was no speed limit and as fast as we were going, cars seemed to be passing us as if we were standing still.

We left the city and came across a part where there were a lot of fields, sheep, cows, and stuff. *Oh, Lord,* I thought. *Please don't let us be stationed near here.* It was just as I feared. We were smack in the middle of the country part of Germany. The base where James was stationed was so small, one could actually stand in the middle of it and see every building on the post. I'm not exaggerating. We did live in military housing in a building that was only for officers, though, which was kind of nice.

After we were settled in, we started meeting people. Of course, our hangout was the officer's club. The officers didn't socialize with the enlisted men, so the same went for the wives. Right away, I noticed something. There were a few (very few) other Black officers, but none of them were married, which meant I was the *only* black officer's wife on *the whole base.*

I sensed trouble and I was right, because a week or so later the wives had a "tea" and I never felt so uncomfortable in my entire life. First of all, all they did was gossip about the wives who weren't there, talk about what their husbands or children recently did that was so funny to them, brag about the nearby cities they visited and what they bought while they were there, and stuff like that. It was like they were all trying to outdo each other. The general's wife was supposed to be the example, or so I thought, but she was the worst one.

Then they all kept staring at me. I guess I did look funny to them by being the only black person besides being the new person, but they didn't have to make it so obvious. They watched every forkful of food I put in my mouth like they were surprised that I even knew how to use a fork, and although there was chatter all around the room, whenever I said something it got so quiet you could hear a pin drop. Talk about culture shock.

When I told James about it, he thought that I was exaggerating. I think deep down he knew it was true, but it was so important to him that I accepted the change because the officer's wives were a direct reflection on their husbands. I guess I understood this, but it didn't make things any easier for me. I was just going through too many "firsts" at one time.

If the control over our social life wasn't hard enough, the weather kept me depressed. Because it was summertime, I had brought only summer clothes with us. The rest of our things were being shipped by the military and they hadn't arrived yet. Almost every day was cold and rainy. All I did all day was clean up, exercise, play with the twins, listen to music, sleep, cry, and think about home. . . .

I started to call home a lot, which was the wrong thing to do, because at that time, international calls cost a lot of money. I called Mom first. It was strange because it was 12:00 midnight but I could hear the theme to a soap opera that I remember came on at

4:00 playing on her TV in the background of our conversation. The first time I called Lydia, she and her sister were so happy that they just screamed in my ear for the first thirty seconds after they realized it was me. I called Medina too, but we mostly wrote to each other, like we'd started doing years before then. I guess that's what I should've done with everybody, because again, at that time, international calls cost a lot of money.

I was happiest when James, the children, and I rode out to nearby cities to sightsee. I was so excited when we went out once and saw a McDonald's. I went off. I ordered a McRib.

"You mean to tell me that out of all the foreign foods here you finally have a chance to try, you want a McRib?" James said as he laughed at me. Once before then, when we were still in the States and were riding out with my mom, James said that he didn't believe they were ribs.

"How can ribs have no bones like that? I think that they're really made of armadillo meat," he kept repeating. Every time he said it, he would put his fingers close together and hold his hands up by his armpits like a dead armadillo beside the road. I thought that it was pretty funny, but Mom said that after she heard James say that, she couldn't eat McRibs for a long time. It didn't stop me, though.

For Christmas, James bought me a ticket to go home. I was so happy to see everybody. The twins were about to turn a year old and it tripped everybody out to see them walking and how big they had grown. As much as I missed James, I have to admit that I loved being back home more.

After a few months, I called James and said I was

ready to return to Germany. James was happy to see me because he said it had started to look like I wasn't coming back. As a matter of fact, he said he refused to believe I was coming back until he actually laid eyes on me. Years later, James said that the first thing I said to him when I got back was that I had just come back to get my things. I can't remember if those were my intentions, but I'll never believe that it was the first thing I told him, because I know that I could have never been that insensitive.

When I got back to Germany, I thought things were finally going to get better, because another black officer was stationed there and about a week or so later, his wife came too. They were okay at first. We got together a lot for dinner and card games. That's when I first learned to play Uno. It wasn't long, though, before the wife started spending more time with the other officers' wives and less time with me. Evidently she "caught on" to the way things were supposed to be. I, on the other hand, just couldn't. I couldn't stand it any longer.

Chapter 18

While walking on post one day, I introduced myself to an enlisted man's wife and we instantly bonded. That was the worst thing I could've done. Later, I understood why it was best that we didn't mingle with them.

The enlisted wife's name was Johnette Seldon. After she became a little more comfortable with me, she felt that she could be honest about her first impression.

"Girl, I remember when you first came to the day care center with your twins. You had your nose all up in the air like you was smelling something."

"Johnette, why you lying on me like that?" I laughed. "I was never that way, so stop lying."

"Yes you did, Ivy. I ain't lying." It seemed that the enlisted men's wives had some kind of preconceived notion that the officers' wives were stuck-up, and I was determined to convince them that although that may have been true about most of them, I was not that way.

Not realizing the damage I was doing, I found

myself associating with more and more of them. Another mistake. This was because Johnette was as sneaky as she could be. She had been married for ten years, which, for some reason, she loved to remind people of, but she loved men. Especially men with money. There was one man in particular whom she was having an affair with, but he wasn't enough. She really wanted to get her hands on an officer. The man she did have the affair with, though, was a good friend of her husband. She used to make her husband think that she couldn't stand the man to throw her husband off. Although I knew I had no business around this kind of stuff, it was the only thing of interest going on.

We always went over to Johnette's house to talk, laugh, eat, and watch her VCR; VCRs were just coming out about that time. Once I rode a bicycle over to her house and stayed too long. When I got ready to go home, it was dark and Johnette kept talking about how several women had been raped in the area around that time. I got scared and stayed over at her house all night. Only thing was she didn't have a phone, so I couldn't call James. He was sick with worry, and when I came home the next morning, it was hard convincing him of what really had happened. About the same time that I finally did finish convincing him of the truth, Johnette came over. She wouldn't come in but stood in the doorway doing a whole lot of whispering and making James suspicious all over again.

Johnette was overall the kind of person who made sure that when the "stuff" hit the fan, she wouldn't be the only one who got splattered. Once, there was another enlisted man's wife whom Johnette fell out with. When they finally faced off, Johnette not only told the woman what she thought of her, but what everybody else was saying about her too, including me. (I hadn't really said anything about the woman, but her husband wasn't too attractive and whenever the other enlisted men's wives laughed at how he looked, I joined in.)

Another messed-up thing Johnette did was try to convince me to call another officer who had an interest in me. I guess she was anxious for me to be in an affair like she was. I felt so uncomfortable because the man was a good friend of James. He had to be, because remember, there were only a few (very few) black officers on that post. Lots of times this officer came over with the other black officers for dinner and cards, and I tried real hard not to make eye contact with him. It was so uncomfortable.

Things got worse and worse between James and me. We started to argue about the twins, money, who would use the car, the phone bill, me hanging with the enlisted wives, everything. At the end of one of the arguments, I finally hit him with the unexpected.

"I want to go back home." He didn't say anything at first but later told me that this was what he expected. He filled out the paperwork but didn't put it in right away in hopes that I would change my mind.

"Can't you stop being selfish long enough to see that you'll be making me look bad if you don't stay?" he'd ask.

"I'm tired of trying to impress these people. After all, *you're* the one in the service, not me. I'm tired of letting these people run my life!" I'd answer.

We continually argued about it, and once, he got

so angry he actually spat in my face. I still remember what he said during our last talk about it.

"Ivy, you need to be sure, because the military pays for only one round-trip ticket for you. The rest of the trips I have to pay for." I looked right in his eyes.

"I *am* sure. I want to go home." Little did I know that when I made that decision, I was also deciding to end my marriage. . . .

Chapter 19

I had just missed Clarita's high school graduation. I would have loved to see her graduate, because I could clearly remember when she very first started going to nursery school. Mom was at work and Liz left for school much earlier than Clarita and I, so on school days, I was the one to wake her, wash her up, comb her hair, give her her breakfast, and put her on her bus. I can even clearly remember her little nursery school graduation ceremony. They looked so cute in their little caps and gowns. Clarita, like the rest of us, always loved to sing. When her class got up to do its selections on the program, Clarita, just like in her church choir today, could be heard over everybody else.

My first conversation with James after I came home was about the other officer. There was no way he could've known unless Johnette had told him. I couldn't believe she did that. Then again, I guess I shouldn't have been surprised. I wrote her three times and asked her why she felt she needed to do that. The last time I wrote her, I told her that if she was *ever* my friend to please write me back. She never answered. I just didn't see why she thought she had to talk to James at all, not unless she thought that he would "cry" on her shoulder.

That same year, Clarita got married. She was a pretty bride. I was a bridesmaid and Mom made all of our dresses. She had about nine bridesmaids in her wedding party, and again, mom made *all* of our dresses. While we marched in, Mom said that because she was having mixed emotions about seeing Clarita get married and she was so tired from making all the dresses, she could do nothing but cry.

Clarita's husband, Alvin, was this big, strapping, country man whom all of us fell in love with as soon as we met him. He was so funny, and there weren't too many things that he took serious. One thing he did take very serious, though, was what he ate. He told Clarita that he didn't want anything out of a box or a can, and because of Alvin, Clarita is the best cook in the family today.

My marriage to James didn't come to an end right away, although it was steadily weakening. It took me a long time to admit this, but it was during this time that I enjoyed the benefits, but not the responsibility, of being married to a military man. I was still very young, immature, and didn't know what was *really* important in life. I loved James, but unfortunately for me, I loved my family and friends more. Until this day, James hasn't forgiven me for feeling this way, in spite of how many times I apologized and told him that if I had a chance to do it again, I would've done it differently. He came home to help me get an apartment, but for some reason, it never felt like home. Before I knew it, I was living with Mom again.

I kept in contact with James, but our calls were becoming farther and farther apart. Eventually, he started dating this German lady and I started dating someone else at home.

After James finished his duty in Germany, his next assignment was back in the States on the East Coast. I kept saying that I was going back to him, but it was only when I was mad at my new love interest, Thomas. I couldn't have gone back to him by this time anyway, because James also had a new love interest and he told me that they were pretty serious. I was happy for him. I really was.

Chapter 20

It was strange the way I hooked up with Thomas. We were working at the same place and he was a little shorter and younger than I was—two things that I ordinarily wouldn't have settled for. But Thomas was far from being an ordinary man. He was strangely quiet and did a lot of talking with his eyes. When he did actually talk, his voice sounded like chocolate tastes. It was smooth and sweet, yet the distinction was strong enough to let you know for sure what it was. Everything about him was attractive, from his smile down to his walk. And the man could dance like nobody's business.

The first time he asked me out we made a date for the movies. I told him to give me a call later that night. I decided to run to the mall and get something new. While at the mall, I heard someone call my name and it was him. You know how sometimes you can be so shocked that you feel like you have to say something, but you don't think before you say it and it comes out sounding stupid?

"How are you going to call me if you're not

home?" I said. I didn't even think of the fact that even if he wasn't home, he still could call me from a public phone. So if he did call, it would be my fault that we didn't talk because I would be the one who wasn't at home. Luckily, though, I don't think he caught on because he was just as shocked to see me as I was him. Later we went to the movies and had a real nice time. That night was the beginning of a four-year relationship.

I fell in love with Thomas's whole family, especially his mom. She was sweetest person I ever met. Until this day, we still have a very close mother-daughter relationship and I can talk to her about anything. Anything.

My mom liked Thomas at first, but that was before she realized how much *I* really liked him.

"What you and that boy putting down, and do you have to see him *every* night?" she asked.

Mom always loved James to no end, even until this day. Years later, she told me that she didn't care *whom* I married—James would *always* be her son-in-law. She felt that I was letting Thomas come between me and James, regardless of how much I tried to convince her that my marriage to James was practically over before Thomas ever came into the picture.

Mom said that Thomas was no longer welcome in her house, so I started to sneak him in while she wasn't home. I felt like I was in high school again. Once when he was there, he forgot his hat. When I went to get it, the hat had disappeared. I know Mom did something with the hat, but until this day, neither one of us has ever said anything about it.

While I was going with Thomas, I ran into Charlotte, another friend from high school. Charlotte wasn't one that hung with us in school, but we talked a lot on the phone. She was always cute in the face, but dressed a little on the homey side. Now, she was gorgeous, and not only did she know it, but she was anxious for everybody else to know it as well. I say this because it was time for our first class reunion.

"Everybody's gonna be shocked when they see me," she kept repeating as she described a red dress she had just bought for the occasion. I, on the other hand, wasn't too anxious to go and finally got up the nerve to tell her. Needless to say, she wasn't too pleased.

Anyway, we started hanging out at the malls almost every Saturday, and on Sundays either she went to church with me or I with her. We had so much fun when we were together doing things like making stupid noises and purposely singing the wrong words to songs we knew, then cracking up at each other. It was as if we were making up for all of the times that we hadn't let ourselves enjoy the friendship that we'd had in high school.

Charlotte and I were very much alike in every way except how we felt about ourselves. She thought that she was pretty and that the world revolved around her. She was so vain, it got on my nerves sometimes, but I still loved this girl like a sister. I, on the other hand, was self-conscious about my weight and the job that I was working at the time. I wasn't too much larger than the average woman; I just felt this way when I was with Charlotte. Regarding my job situation, up to this time I'd always had a job that barely paid over minimum wage. I knew that this was because of either my education level or my refusal to stay on a job long enough to get raises. I always felt that even though I didn't graduate from college, the time that I did go overqualified me for certain jobs. I would take a job because I needed it so much at the moment; then, after working it for only a short time, I would be unhappy with it because either it didn't pay that much or it wasn't what I really wanted to do. Eventually, I'd use the slightest excuse to quit. What I didn't think about was that if I stayed on the job, even without a lot of education, I still would eventually make more money. (I recently had a job where the manager didn't even finish high school and was making $50,000 annually. This may not be a lot of money to some, but it is for a high school dropout.) Liz used to get on me all the time about "job hopping" the way I did.

"Let me tell you something, Ivy. A lot of times I'm not happy with everything and everybody on my job, either, but I know I got to take the bitter with the sweet to keep it. Girl, please, you ain't suppose to let *nothing* run you from your money. *Nothing.*" By this time, she had been at her job for about six years. Today, about thirty years and several promotions later, she's at the very same job.

Anyway, Thomas couldn't stand Charlotte because he said that I spent too much time with her and always forgot about him. One time, he wanted to see me and I told him that I couldn't because I didn't have a babysitter for the twins. This was *after* my mom said she would baby-sit so that I could go out with Charlotte. When Thomas called me a few minutes later just to talk, I was gone. Charlotte and I went to a college basketball game at the Hampton Coliseum. We sat right behind the goal. After the game, I felt so guilty that I went to see Thomas. He was up watching TV. I knew something was wrong as soon as he opened the door and looked at me.

"What's up?" he asked, then turned and walked away.

"What's wrong?" I asked him.

"I called you and your mom said that you wasn't home."

"I have something to tell you," I softly said. Over his shoulder, I could see the 11:00 news coming on.

"I'm waiting," Thomas said, not taking his eyes off mine.

"I lied to you."

"Why, Ivy?"

"So that I could go out with Charlotte." On the news, the sports highlights started showing.

"I don't see why you felt like you had to lie."

"Because I know how much you hate her, Thomas. And I didn't want you to be mad at me whenever I go somewhere with her." My heart started racing because every time they showed the ball going in the basket, they also showed Charlotte and me.

"And you don't think that lying to me makes me mad?"

"I know it does and I'm sorry, Thomas. I'm really sorry. . . ." Thomas was too much into our conversation to notice what was on TV and, boy, was I glad. I still wasn't in the clear, though, because as soon as I got home, Mom started in on me.

"Why you lie so much, Ivy?"

"What, Ma?"

"You told me that you was going out with Charlotte. That's what, Ma."

"That ain't no lie. I *did* go out with Charlotte," I said, feeling like I was thirteen years old again.

"Why would she call here looking for you if ya'll was together, Ivy?"

"Because I made a stop before I came back home."

"Yeah, I bet you *did* make a stop before you came back home. You ought to stop that mess, Ivy." I went in my mom's room and called Charlotte.

"Girl, you got me in trouble! I stopped by Thomas's after I dropped you off and now Mom don't believe that I was with you!"

"Oh, I'm sorry, girl," Charlotte said, laughing. "I just wanted to see if you saw us on the news!"

The only thing I hated about Charlotte was that *she* was the big liar. Again, I'm not trying to judge anybody, because I know I'm in no position to do that. I used to tell a hot one every now and then too, but it was mostly when I was trying to get myself out of some kind of trouble. Charlotte, on the other hand, used to lie just to be lying. She hurt my feelings so bad once when I baby-sat her children for her. Thomas got mad because Michael and Michelle were with James's parents for the weekend.

"What kind of sense do it make for you to have a babysitter for your own children, and then baby-sit someone else's?" he asked.

"I don't know. I just promised her that I would and I don't want to go back on my word," I slowly answered. Thomas shook his head, walked away, and didn't say too much more to me for the whole weekend.

When the weekend was finally over and Charlotte came to pick her children up, it had started to rain. I put Michelle's raincoat on her daughter so that she wouldn't get wet. A few weeks passed by, but I didn't say anything else about the coat because it hadn't rained again. About a month or so later, the weather reporters predicted a terrible storm. That same day, the wind started blowing real hard and the schools were closing early. Before I picked up Michelle from school, I stopped by Charlotte's house to pick up the raincoat. She told me that it wasn't there, because she had come by my house sometime earlier and given it to Thomas. I said okay and left. When I saw Thomas again, I asked him why he didn't tell me that Charlotte had come by and given him Michelle's raincoat.

"What you say?" he asked, with his face frowned.

"Why didn't you tell me that Charlotte came by and gave you Michelle's raincoat?" I repeated.

"What did you say, Ivy?" Thomas asked me again. This time I knew that he had heard what I said and I started to smell something funny, but I asked him once more anyway.

"Ivy, you know good and well as much as I can't stand that girl, I would've told you if she came by here and gave me *anything*."

I just stood there stunned with a stupid look on my face. He took full advantage of the opportunity to rub it in that Charlotte still had the coat and had lied to me about giving it back.

"But that's your *friend*, right?"

About two to three weeks went by before I could bring myself to say anything to her about the coat. Even though she had lied about it, I probably would've let her keep it if *I* had bought it. That's just how much I hated confronting her about it. Although I was full grown by then and didn't have to physically fight to prove a point like we did when we were children, I still was a weakling when it came to defending myself. I've just always hated confrontation, even to this day. The thing about the coat was that my mom bought it. The year was 1985, when the Cabbage Patch dolls were popular, so it was a real cute little pink coat that had the Cabbage Patch kids on it.

The next time Charlotte and I went to the mall, I had to really boost myself to ask her about it. I don't know if she had forgotten what she had previously told me, but what she was telling me right then wasn't the same thing.

"I brought it over to your house and sent Jerry [her son] to the door with it, and—"

I cut her off. "That's not what you told me before. . . ."

"Huh?"

It was taking so much out of me to finish the confrontation that I could hardly stand it, but I was determined to do it because I knew that I wasn't the one who was wrong.

"You told me that *you* gave it to Thomas."

Charlotte then tried to make believe that she didn't know exactly what had happened. When I couldn't take it any longer, I just put her, and myself, out of our misery.

"Don't worry about it. I'll just get it on the way home." From the time I had first run back into Charlotte from high school until then, it was the longest and quietest ride we'd ever had together. When I dropped her off, she went in and got the coat and gave it to me. I said thanks. Nothing else was ever said about it. Ever.

Thomas said that she was a liar and I was crazy for still having anything else to do with her because she'd eventually hurt me again, but I refused to believe it. I just loved her too much.

Chapter 21

As time passed, I got another apartment. This one felt a lot more at home, because as much as I respected my mother and her house, I was so tired of living like I was in high school. . . .

I had recently received divorce papers from James. Among other things, the papers stipulated that I was no longer to have his last name, I wasn't to receive any of his military retirement benefits, and he would pay a total of $400 a month for child support. I totally ignored the part about no longer using his last name. Not because I thought it was so great, like "Kennedy" or "Rockefeller," like he must have thought, but because I didn't want my last name to be different from my children's.

I wasn't surprised when I got the divorce papers, because it seemed that James's relationship with his new love interest on the East Coast was even more serious than I'd thought, and I suppose he was trying to prepare for another marriage.

By this time James had been promoted to captain. I was happy for him. I really was. We still kept in contact so I could report the progress of the twins. All the information James didn't get from me, he got from his father, who was always *very* involved with the twins. Lots of times when I went to the neighborhood grocery or drugstore, I would hear James's father's voice hollering across the store to me, "Where da babies?"

Before I knew it, it was time for the twins to start school. They were only four years old and in the First Step program. I'll never forget their first day. They looked so small climbing onto that big yellow bus, dressed just alike and lunch boxes in hand—"He-Man" for Michael and "Cabbage Patch" for Michelle. I cried on my way back home from their bus stop, and when I got there, I called Mom. She laughed, then told me that I knew they had to go sooner or later and assured me that they would be okay.

The same personalities that the twins showed when the nurse first brought them to me in the hospital held true, and have continued even to this day. When I bought them their first little board games like Chutes and Ladders, Candy Land, and Hi Ho! Cherry-O, I usually stayed in another room and listened to them play. When Michael would take a turn and it would put him too far ahead of Michelle, he would let Michelle take another turn so that she could catch up. However, if the shoe was on the other foot, Michelle took no pity on Michael. Sometimes I wouldn't say anything; sometimes I would.

At their school, I had to request that they not be in the same class, because of the teacher's concerns.

"They are too involved with each other's progress, which isn't a good thing."

"Besides, Michelle bosses Michael around far too much," the teachers would add. I knew it was true from how I'd seen them interact at home.

"Ma, I am going to audition for the school play," Michael announced to me one day when he came home. He sounded so cute when he talked, taking his time to pronounce each word precisely to the letter.

"That's good," I answered, my mind probably preoccupied with something else.

About a week later, he came back to me and said, "Ma, I am in the school play."

"What's the name of the play, Michael?"

"The Man Who Loved to Laugh," he answered.

"And what part do you have?"

"The Man Who Loved to Laugh," he repeated. I called Mom and told her and we both cracked up.

James married the girl he had started dating. I had mixed feelings about it, because something told me that she really didn't love him but was only impressed by the money she "thought" he had. However, I couldn't tell him this without sounding like I was jealous, so I just didn't say anything.

Eventually, just like I thought he would, he started acting funny about helping me with the twins. I had mixed feelings about this too. I knew that he had a new life, but at the same time, I felt that his first responsibility was to the twins.

The thing that hurt me most was the way James and his new wife treated me once when the twins' military ID cards had expired and I called James to ask him about it. His new wife answered the phone and told me that he wasn't home. I asked her if she would please tell him to call me when he got there and she said that she would. About an hour later, not James, but the new wife called back.

"Hello?"

"Hello, Ivy?"

"Yes?"

"This is Juanita. Do you know who I am?"

Naw, I never heard of you in my life, you dip.

"Yes, I know who you are," I said.

"Well, your check is in the mail, so there's no need for you to call here anymore."

I was watching Oprah Winfrey, and this day, her show was real good. It was one show where someone in the audience had said something about putting on her "Oprah Winfrey wig" and Oprah didn't know that there was such a thing. My girl Oprah was too upset, and as much as I hated to miss what she was going to do about it, I jumped up and turned down the volume.

"What'd you say?"

"I *said,* 'Your check is in the mail.'"

I was so shocked, I didn't say anything. This wench had a lot of nerve.

"Did you hear me?" she was saying.

Are you out of your very mind? Didn't you know that man had children before you married him? I ain't calling 'bout no John Brown check, because that nigger know what I'll do if he don't send my mess on time. For your information, I was calling about the twins' ID cards, you imbecile!

"Yeah, I heard you."

When we hung up, I was too upset. I called Mom, who said that although Juanita was wrong for doing that, that's how second wives were about first wives calling their house and I should've expected it. Believe it or not, though, that's not the part that had me upset. What made me really mad was that the next time I talked to James, he told me that he was standing right beside Juanita when she made the call. He said Juanita tried to make him do it but he wouldn't (like that was supposed to make him look good or something), so she did it herself.

Another time James called me talking trash about getting some more of my "stuff," and when Juanita came in, he hung up on me. I started to dial him back but decided against it. Right then I decided what I was going to tell him whenever we talked again: "I think it's so funny that you married someone that you're afraid of."

In my mind, I did think it was funny. In my heart, I didn't. . . .

About the same time this happened, my very closest friends were Lydia and her sister, Charlotte; Gloria; Mildred; and of course Medina. Medina was the only one whom I didn't see on a regular basis, because she had finally moved from Virginia back to her home state, New York, but our letter writing never stopped. She swore that reading my letters was just as entertaining as reading an *Essence* magazine, and she actually had to sit alone in a quiet place with a cup of coffee while she read them. She timed her move back home perfectly, because very soon afterwards she ran into one of her old boy-friends. They had started dating again and gotten married. She was so happy and deserved every bit of it. A little while after they were married, I went to visit them. I took the plane. Although it was only my fourth plane ride, I felt like a pro, because my first three had been overseas. I had a ball. Just when I decided that these six women were the best friends in the world, I met Johnice.

Johnice and I met at the job where we both worked. Johnice was a lot like me when it came to laughing, playing, and harmlessly picking on people, but she was very serious about her salvation. Her husband was a deacon in their church and she was a deaconess. We bonded instantly.

I guess it sounds like I bonded instantly with a lot of people, but believe it or not, I was very particular in choosing friends. In the workplace, though, it was important to me that there wasn't a whole lot of childish stuff going on all the time—like this one doesn't like that one, that one isn't speaking to this one, and this one said something about that one—so I always acted up, making people laugh all the time to keep the mess down and the workplace happy. It just seemed to make the workday go smoother when everyone was happy and at ease. Because I acted like that, though, it drew people to me. Most of them I just dealt with at work, but every so often I would get close to someone and spend time with that person outside of the workplace as well. Sometimes, I didn't even know why. I guess God had something to do with it.

I know that was the case with Johnice, because I talked to her a lot (when we weren't acting the fool) and she witnessed to me, telling me that maybe I was going through what I was going through because I had forgotten about God, and she showed me the scripture in the Bible about returning to my first love. I knew she was right, but at the time I just didn't want to hear it. I changed my seat at work, but it did no good, because there was an empty seat behind me and Johnice moved right in it.

One Sunday Johnice invited me to go to church with her and I went. Her husband was the speaker on that Sunday, and although I can't remember everything he said, he closed with a description of Jesus dying on the cross for us.

"Can you see him?" he kept repeating. When the alter call was made, I went up and rededicated my life to God.

The job where Johnice and I worked was a production job where we sewed burlap bags for agricultural businesses and we were paid strictly by how many bags we could produce. The other ladies who worked in our section couldn't stand us, because on a daily average, we could make twice the requirement (or more), and still had time to laugh, talk about God's goodness, and eat. Oh, my Lord, did we eat.

We weren't supposed to be eating at our workstations, so the women brought little stuff like crackers, cookies, chips, and other things that they could easily sneak to eat. Johnice and I, on the other hand, went out to lunch and brought back steaming-hot, full-course plates of food with knives and forks just like we were sitting down at a dinner table or something. It was stuff like fried chicken, pork chops, meat loaf, and the whole nine, including peach cobbler for dessert. The other workers would look over there where we were, because they knew they were smelling food, but they could never catch us. We were too good. Besides, it wasn't them we had to hide from anyway, but the supervisors.

Although the supervisors told us that we weren't supposed to eat, deep down I don't think they really cared. I think they just didn't want us to get food on the bags. Every once in a while when one of us made a big mistake and the client would send the bags back, the head supervisor would call us all to the middle of the floor for what we called a powwow and get at us about it. Once when he called us for a powwow, he had a bag that was returned because there was a chicken bone sewn in it. When we went back to our machines, Johnice and I didn't say a word, just went back to sewing like our very lives depended on it.

One of our supervisors, Brandon Robinson, was real cool. He was the only black supervisor there. Johnice and I talked and laughed with him all the time. The only thing wrong with that was when Brandon got serious with us about something we weren't supposed to be doing and started fussing at us, we'd fuss back at him. We knew how far to go, though—trust me. We weren't crazy; we knew that Brandon could get us out of there just like the white supervisors could if push came to shove.

Johnice was also in beauty school. When we weren't talking trash or about the goodness of the Lord, I was helping her study. Yes, helping her study her beauty school lesson while we were supposed to be working, and we *still* got the work done. There was always something to look forward to while working with Johnice. She tried to get me to go to beauty school with her, but at the time I just didn't want to. Many times since then, I wished that I had, because today, Johnice is one of the best hairdressers in the city and owns her own beauty parlor. Sometimes I can't help but wonder that if I had gone to beauty school with her, would I have gotten that far. I am so proud of her.

The next time Medina and her new family came to visit me, she had three children. We enjoyed each other's company like never before. One of the things Medina and I did while her husband volunteered to stay home with the children, was go to see Luther Vandross at King's Dominion. All the way home, we sang Luther songs. When we started singing "Wait for Love," we got into a disagreement about one of the lines. We kept singing it over and over the way we thought it was supposed to be until we got tired of trying to figure it out, then we started singing anything that came to our minds. We were cracking up.

A little while later I visited Medina again. This time I took the bus and didn't tell her that I was coming. During the last transfer, I got lost and had to call her and ask her what to do next.

"Where are you now?" she asked.

"I don't know!" I answered. "That's why I'm calling you! Wait, there's a couple near me. Let me ask them," I said. The couple told me where I was, but they were looking at me real funny. When I finally got to Medina's and was telling her about the couple, she said the reason they were looking at me like that was that they were probably thieves and thought that I was an undercover cop trying to set them up.

"Lord have mercy." I laughed. "I'm glad they did think that, because if they knew that I wasn't a cop, they would've got me for everything I had!"

Chapter 22

James and his new wife moved back to Virginia about a half hour away from me. He was discharged from the service. He said he wanted to be close to the children. I do believe that, but I don't think that was the only reason he got out.

Right before he moved back to Virginia, I started having a lot of trouble with him paying child support. He just stopped. I found out about an office at the local military post where I could complain about it, so I did. I just didn't think it was fair that he was leaving me to take care of the twins by myself like that. I suppose he thought that since he had this new "life," the twins had just disappeared or just didn't need any food, clothing, or shelter anymore.

James must've talked to his father about this too, because one time his father came over to my place and really let me have it about how I had messed up my and James's relationship and now that James had someone else with whom he was happy and I was trying to mess that up too, I was going to get it back.

His father thought a lot of me and had never talked to me like that before, and I was so hurt that I almost decided to leave James alone and try to make it by myself. Almost. I asked my mom and Medina whether I was wrong. They both said no and not to let up.

James finally admitted that my complaining about him not paying child support also had something to do with him getting out of the army. I immediately thought about one of the conversations that we'd previously had.

"I'll just get out of the army before I live under your thumb like this," he had said.

"Do what you gotta do, James, but trust me, you'll be hurting no one but yourself. . . ." I had answered. I really thought it was sad that he would have rather walked away from such a promising career, than help take care of his children.

I didn't know why he got out and it wasn't even important at that point. All I knew was that I was determined that he was going to help me take care of those twins in one way or another. . . .

I'll never forget the time when the twins were outside playing and Michael came back inside crying with his mouth all bloody. He said that the boy he was playing with promised him that he could ride his Big Wheel if he pushed the boy on it first. If you can remember how the Big Wheel was made, the seat was very low to the ground. While Michael was pushing the boy, his hands slipped off the back of it and he fell on his face. When I first saw Michael I got scared, but when I cleaned his face I saw that it was no more than the usual busted lip that a child gets when he or she falls. About an hour later, though, Michael was still crying just as hard as he was when he first came in the house. He never made a fuss like that when he fell before, so I started thinking that maybe he was hurt worse than I realized.

"Mike!"

"Y-y-yes?"

"Come here." He slowly came in the room where I was, looking down.

"Y-y-yes?"

"Your mouth *still* hurt?"

"No," he answered.

"Then why are you still crying like that?" I asked.

"Because I never got to *ride* it," he answered, with his little hands turned up to help him explain. I felt like someone had just stabbed me in my heart with a butcher's knife and started turning it real slow. I just thought it was a shame that Michael was crying about a ride on someone else's Big Wheel like that when his father was a captain in the U.S. Army. It was at that very point that I decided I would work any job I had to, short of breaking the law, to get some of the things the twins *wanted* and not just what they *needed*. I was determined that one day we would have a nice house with a big backyard and they would have lots of toys, including a swing set, which is what I always wanted as a child and never got.

James's new wife wasn't too happy with their move to Virginia, or so I gathered from what eventually happened. James had a bachelor's degree, which enabled him to get a management position with a company, but that wasn't good enough for Miss Hoity Toity because let us not forget, she married a captain in the army. She hung in there for a little while, and then she was gone. Later, James told me that she supposedly "hooked up" with a professional basketball player. Anyway, he didn't take her leaving too well. I mean he *really* didn't take it too well. I mean he *really, really* didn't take it too well. . . .

Chapter 23

Eventually, my grandmother got sick. She had a stroke, but I think it was mainly old age taking over. She was about eighty-five years old.

Grandma was a very spry woman, even in her old age. Her name was Pearl and she looked just like her name. She always dressed real frisky and had a personality to match. Whatever she wore, she had to have the stockings, shoes, pocketbook, beads, and earbobs to match. That's what she called her necklaces and earrings, beads and earbobs. Oh, and don't forget the strap shoes. That's what she called sandals. Strap shoes. My mom told me that one time Grandma said that she didn't want a pocketbook with two straps, because they were for "old people." Sure enough, I started noticing that the pocketbooks carried by younger women had only one strap, and the older women's bags usually had two. Even until this day, I still notice it usually being that way.

My mom, uncles, and aunts decided it was best that Grandma be in a nursing home so that she

would have the twenty-four-hour care that she
needed. I didn't like to go to the nursing home, because those people in there were so pitiful, it used
to make me almost cry. Once when we were there
visiting Grandma, another old lady came up to the
doorway of Grandma's room in a wheelchair.

"Come on and take me to the store." All of us
stopped talking and just looked at each other, not
knowing what to say.

"Come on now," the lady kept repeating until she
got tired and left. I guess she went to ask somebody
else. I felt so sorry for her.

We would also hear other people in other rooms
crying for help but no one would go to see about
them. I guess at the nursing home things like that
go on all the time; the nurses who work there "hear
and don't hear" them. But what I wonder is, how do
they know when the patients seriously need their
help? I don't know; it just all seems so sad to me, but
I guess those people have to go somewhere. Especially when their family members have jobs and families that they have to take care of and can't give
them the twenty-four-hour attention that they need.

Grandma was there for about two weeks when I
got a call from Mom.

"She's gone." I hung up the phone and started to
scream. Michelle came in and gave me a hug.

Grandma knew a lot of people and her funeral was
evidence of it. Bishop Edison captured Grandma's
spry personality perfectly in the eulogy. He took his
text from the Song of Solomon. When he read the
part about "leaping across the mountains and bounding across the hills," he said he could just see my
grandma dressed all pretty as she did just that into her

afterlife. As I closed my eyes I could see it too. . . . She had on a pink flowered dress, a wide-brim straw hat with a pink scarf tied around it and hanging down her back, some pink strap shoes, and some pearl beads and earbobs. In her hand she carried a tiny pink purse with one strap. . . .

Chapter 24

My relationship with Thomas had finally come to an end and I was hurt. It wasn't long before he started dating someone else, but I often still visited his house, because his mother and I had become very close. Whenever I went over there, I was hoping that Thomas would be there, and most of the time he was. We'd have long talks that always resulted in us deciding it was best that we stay broken up. Eventually I got over the breakup and made myself content with just being his friend, although he still was very special to me. Before we broke up, though, we made plans to go to a Luther Vandross concert, so we still went. When Luther sang "Superstar," Thomas held my hand real tight. I knew that we would always hold a special place in each other's heart. Always . . .

I didn't stay "single" long, because Brandon, the cool supervisor where I worked, wanted me to meet a "friend" of his. To be perfectly honest, I wasn't looking to be in another relationship at that time, although I figured it would be kind of nice to go out to dinner or a movie with the opposite sex every now and then.

Vincent *seemed* nice. He was tall, nice looking, and well mannered. He was the first man I ever went out with who opened and closed the car door for me. I didn't think that men actually did that anymore.

For our first date, we went to the skating rink. I was too afraid to get on skates, because it had been so long for me, so he skated alone. I was glad I didn't go out there with him, because this man could *really* skate. I just sat on the side and watched him. Every time he passed me, he gave me the sweetest smile. When he finished skating, he went to the game machines, won a stuffed animal, and snuck up behind me to surprise me with it. I had a good time.

What stood out the most about Vincent was that he *seemed* to love the Lord. We shared our opinion with each other on the Bible and different churches' beliefs. Conversation with Vincent was always good.

Eventually we started to spend more and more time together and I started to care for him more than I realized. His main job just happened to be very close to where I lived, so it wasn't long before he was coming over almost every day and having dinner with me and the twins.

I found myself talking about him a lot to Johnice and Charlotte, the two people whom I talked to the most at that time. My and Medina's letter collection was steadily growing as I kept her posted too. They all usually were very encouraging when I talked to them about Vincent. When we had a good date, they'd say something like, "Maybe your relationship will grow into a more serious one." But when we had a bad date, they'd say something like, "Forget that nigger, because he isn't worth the trouble." We had more good dates than bad ones, though, so I was hopeful. . . .

Vincent was also involved with a fast-growing business as a part-time job. It was the type of business where the more people he brought into it, the better things were for him because he was paid for their work as well as his own. Of course, I had started going to his business meetings with him and helping him think of other people whom we could visit, tell about the business, and possibly bring into the business as well.

Even though we had been spending a lot of time together, Vincent wasn't showing anything more than just a "friendly" interest in me, so I finally gave up on any hopes of having a serious relationship with him. At first it bothered me, but later I figured it was like apples and oranges. By this I mean that although both fruits are equally good, one fruit is preferred over the other. I figured that although I was a good apple, maybe Vincent just preferred oranges. Even so, he still came over a lot to hang out and we still worked on the business together.

One night I invited Charlotte to the business meeting with us. (As the pastor of the church I used to belong to would often say, "You see where I'm going with this?") Eventually Vincent's visits and Charlotte's phone calls slowed down at the same time although it wasn't enough for me to notice because I still continued to call Charlotte every day.

One day at work, Brandon told me that Vincent had gotten engaged. I was so shocked I almost fell out of my chair. I called another mutual friend of Vincent's and mine named Bryan.

"Are you sitting down?"

"Yeah."

"Guess who's engaged?"

"Who?"

"Vincent."

Then Bryan said to me, "Are *you* sitting down?"

"Yeah."

"Guess who he's engaged *to?*"

"Who?"

"Charlotte."

"Hang up." Bryan knew me for a long time and knew what I was getting ready to do.

"Wait a minute, Ivy. Don't—"

"Hang up!"

"At least wait until you cool down, Ivy. Please don't—"

"I *am* cool. I'm just gonna ask her why couldn't she tell me herself, that's all."

"Okay. Call me right back after ya'll hang up."

You know how when you're on the phone and you're so in a rush to talk to the next person that you don't hang up, you just push the button down with your finger? Well, that's just what I did.

"Hey."

"Hey, girl. What's up?"

"Guess who's engaged?"

"Who?"

"Guess."

"Liz?"

"Nope."

"Lydia?"

"Nope."

"Who?"

"Guess!"

I can't remember who else's name she called, but Charlotte listed at least six more people, and I'm not exaggerating. Keep in mind now, I had talked to this girl about Vincent every day for at least a year. At least. However, she called the name of everybody else whom we both knew *except* his.

"Stop playing, girl, and tell me who's engaged," I said.

"Who?"

"Vincent."

"Oh yeah?"

"Yeah, girl. Ain't that a trip?"

"How'd you find that out?"

"I can't remember," I lied, "but whoever she is, she must be something else."

Silence.

I decided to put her out of her misery (again) and told her I'd talk to her later and hung up.

I called everybody I could think of, and each person was just as shocked as I was. Almost.

"Girl, you better *shut up!*"

"Ivy, stop lying!"

"What? Ain't that some shit?"

"I ain't *never* trusted her; she always seemed sneaky to me."

"Give me her number so *I* can cuss that heifer out!"

"I can't believe she did that long as ya'll been friends. . . ."

"*Charlotte?*"

I thought about Thomas's prediction that he had made about a year earlier. Although I thought he would rub it in my face, I called him anyway. He didn't rub it in my face.

"Dag, that was messed up," was all he said.

When I got myself together, I called Charlotte back.

"I found out who he is engaged to."

"Who?"

I couldn't believe that she was still playing games, but I didn't want to play anymore.

"Charlotte, why didn't you tell me?"

"Ivy, I didn't know how to tell you."

"Why?"

Silence.

"Charlotte?"

"Ivy, he said what ya'll had wasn't serious."

"Charlotte, how he felt about me wasn't even the issue—you knew how *I* felt about *him* and the closeness you and I had shouldn't have allowed you to get involved with him."

Silence.

"Charlotte?"

"Are you saying that I betrayed our friendship?"

Silence.

"Charlotte, all I can say is that I don't know how I will feel later, but right now I can't be happy for you."

"I understand."

"I'll talk to you later." (Little did I know how much later it really was going to be.)

"Bye."

I guess all is fair in love and war, but I'm also a firm believer in what goes around, comes around. . . .

Charlotte and Vincent were married early that next year and had three children. Three. I kept thinking about her. In spite of everything that had happened, I still loved Charlotte, and for the life of me I couldn't understand why. People use that phrase "for the life of me" all the time, but I really mean it whenever I use it. If someone were actually standing over me to take my very life if I didn't give him or her the answer to whatever he or she was asking me, that person would have to take my life.

I eventually started having bad feelings and dreams about Charlotte. I wanted so bad to ask her if she was okay, but I didn't know how to contact her. My bad feelings and dreams were right, because it wasn't long before I started hearing from *very* reliable sources that Vincent was treating her bad—not holding a job, cheating on her, and even fighting with her until they eventually broke up. People who knew of our situation said it served her right. In my mind, I felt the same. In my heart, I didn't. . . .

Thomas married the girl he was dating. I called him and sung "Congratulations" by Vesta. We both laughed.

Everything was happening all at once. If I could just get away and start over, I would be okay. At least that's what I thought. . . .

Chapter 25

There were several people who weren't too pleased with my decision to move from Virginia. Of course, Mom didn't feel too good about it. Bishop Edison wasn't too happy either, because at that time, I was doing a lot of work with the youth department at our church. I was the youth choir director and a Sunday school teacher. I had even started helping with the senior choir too. Bishop Edison called me in his office before I left.

"What about the children?" he asked. I couldn't even give him an answer. He prayed for me and wished me well. He was the best pastor I ever had.

I was trying to think of the best way to tell James I was leaving, but he found out before I got a chance. Until this day he resents me for "taking the children out of his life," but I don't see it that way because I never closed the door on his communication with the twins. Never. I just didn't see why I had to stay where I was no longer happy when there were so many different means of communication and transportation in the world. Nevertheless, when I moved, all communication between James and the children stopped. Child support and all.

The year was 1990, and I was thirty-two years old. I moved to New York where Medina lived. We were both so excited because after all we'd been through together—sharing the house off campus while going to Virginia State, visiting each other after we moved out of the house, me visiting her after I dropped out of school, her making up my face for my wedding, her visiting me when I had the twins, her calling me and writing letters of encouragement when I was in Germany, her visiting me with her new family and then she and I going to the Luther Vandross concert, me visiting her and her new family, and us writing the many letters to each other during all this time—we ended up as next door neighbors. It had been about ten years since we first met, but it seemed like we knew each other all of our lives. We were so close that we felt like sisters, and to all who didn't know any better, that's how we introduced ourselves.

The twins had a hard time adjusting, because as a general rule, children are mean. Of course, the first issue was their southern accent. I thought about Freda and Nicky. I guess this was understandable, though. Maybe kids aren't mean. Maybe they're just honest. They say whatever's on their mind if they're not taught to respect the feelings of others. And even if they *are* taught, they speak before they think in most cases. It didn't take the twins long to adjust, though. *I'm* the one who had a hard time, even though I thought I wouldn't.

I got a job right away, but I had to go through three before I found one that I was happy with. Still something was missing—I had to find a church.

We visited one church, but it was too slow. I saw one of the ladies, who was at the church we visited, on the street. We got into a conversation about the church I went to at home, and she told me of another church that sounded more like what we were looking for. I took the twins that following Sunday, and sure enough, we fell in love with it. If anything made me unhappy with it at first, it was the fact that it was bigger than the church we came from. Not a whole lot, just enough to make me uncomfortable. I would say that it had about twice the membership. I was never too fond of a big church, but it was okay because the way I figured, the bigger it was, the harder it would be for everybody to be into everybody else's business. Or so I thought.

There was always something to do there. The choir was the bomb. The pastor's oldest son played the keyboard, his youngest son played the lead guitar, his nephew played the bass guitar, and his other nephew played the drums. I'm telling ya'll, these guys were so good, they sounded just like professionals. I couldn't wait to join.

The children had a choir that was good too. Just like with the adult choir, the members were taught to sing in all three parts: soprano, alto, and tenor. The pastor's daughter picked up kids in the neighborhood for rehearsals. This was a good thing for the kids, because otherwise, they probably never would've gone to church. When they had to sing or do some other type of program, they would invite their parents to see them. This was a good thing for the parents for the same reason.

I really liked the pastor's daughter. She was always doing something with the children of the church, which was right down my line. She was the youth leader at the church, as well as a teacher at the local elementary school. I can't remember if I ever told her this, but she's the one who made me seriously re-think going back to school to complete my educa-tion. I always wished that I had finished, but before meeting her, that's all it was—something I *wished* that I had done. After watching her work with those chil-dren, hearing her talk about her job as a school-teacher, and seeing her love for working with children in general, I knew that I had that same love and that it was time for me to do something about it.

Soon I joined the church and started to sing with the choir and work closely with the pastor's daugh-ter in the youth department. The pastor's daughter could see that I had the same "fire" that she did when it came to the children, and soon I was head-ing different programs for the children as well. I loved it. What made me so happy was that the twins loved it too, because it was real important to me to make the twins as happy as possible with the move.

Every summer, the youth department in the church had some kind of conference where a lot of the congregations of visiting churches came to-gether, and at the end of the conference, the youth leaders along with the children did a play. They were awesome. Once, we even used the local high school so that we could have the full effect of the stage lights, smoke machines to create fog, and other things to make the play more realistic.

Every Christmas, the little children did a play by themselves. The first time I saw this I was amazed, because these plays weren't just a few lines that the kids had to remember and most of the time forgot, but plays of full scripts that lasted anywhere from a half hour to a full hour. Those kids knew what was expected of them and did just that.

Michael and Michelle fell right in, and I was so proud of them, because besides singing with the choir and learning to sing in parts, taking part in the plays, and whatever else they did, Michael and Michelle were the most respectful children in the church. I'm not saying this because they were *my* children, but because it's true. Even if I didn't think so, too many other people were saying it for it to be a lie.

As I closed my eyes and smiled, the good memories and the warm feelings were on their way from my mind to my heart, then Anger tapped me on my shoulder reminding me of the bad ones. I knew it was too good to be true.

The first thing that upset me while going to the church was the way I was betrayed when I had lunch with the pastor's wife and confided in her about some things I was going through that had me somewhat depressed. A little later I had a conversation with her sister, and this sister repeated everything that I had told the pastor's wife. I mean word for word. I guess I shouldn't have been surprised, though, for three reasons. First, usually when a "new" person comes around, people are anxious to know everything about that person, especially the dirt. Second, ladies, for some reason, love to gossip. Some men do too, but we ladies have them hands down. And third, she told her *sister*. You're supposed to feel that you can trust your sister when you don't feel that you can trust anyone else, so I seriously doubt that she thought her sister would tell anyone else what was said, especially *me*.

The second thing that upset me was something that happened with one of the pastor's nephews. The pastor had three sisters who also went to the church and one of them had a son who was a couple of years older than Michelle.

This son was very nice looking, if I say so myself, and could sing and play the drums like nobody's business. Anyway, Michelle had just reached the age (about nine or ten) where she didn't think boys were "yucky" anymore and had a crush on this boy. One day a lady in the church called me and told me that her granddaughter said that Michelle and this boy had supposedly done something they had no business doing. I can't remember if she said that her granddaughter told her directly or that she heard some of the other little girls from the church, who were visiting her granddaughter, talking about it. Nevertheless, I was upset and asked Michelle about it. She started crying as she told me that they had kissed and he had touched her privates.

Don't misunderstand; I didn't blame the boy, because I'm more than sure that he didn't force Michelle to do it, but I still felt that it should have been addressed. We (Michelle, the boy, his mom, and I) all ended up in the pastor's office to talk about what had happened. The boy denied it all and said that nothing had ever happened. Nothing. I didn't take my eyes off Michelle, who never looked up and had started to cry. I knew that there was no way that she would've embarrassed herself like that if it were not true. Keep in mind now, this boy's mom was the pastor's sister.

I didn't have a car at the time, so after the meeting the pastor and his wife gave us a ride home, as they had several times in the past. All the other times we talked and laughed all the way, but this time the whole ride was silent. When we got home, the pastor turned to me and said something that I couldn't believe.

"Now don't worry about this, Sister Ivy. Hold your head up, because we've had previous trouble with that boy being dishonest, and [just like I was thinking] there is no way Michelle would've taken herself through all that had it not been true."

You mean you knew *he was lying and didn't say so in the meeting when you saw how Michelle was hurting?* I thought but didn't have the courage to say. I was so upset that I wanted to leave the church, but the twins didn't want to, so I stayed.

To make matters worse, Mom called that night to say that my Aunt Mary had died. . . .

Eventually, I started to get lonely and depressed and to miss home a lot. Soon I started dating again. The guy's name was John and what I liked most about him was his intelligence. He worked in one of the city office buildings and I had never actually dated a businessman like him before.

Long before I started dating John, I had mentioned to another lady who went to the same church and also worked at the same place that I did that there was a city bus driver whom I liked to talk to whenever I rode the bus. She told me that the bus driver was married. I didn't see what that had to do with anything, because I had no romantic interest in this man. I just liked talking to him when I rode the bus, as I had noticed that many others also did.

Naturally, when I started dating John, the people of the church wanted to know who he was and I wouldn't say. The lady whom I mentioned the bus driver to assumed it was the bus driver and mentioned it to one of the pastor's sisters. The rumor spread like a brushfire. By the time all this had happened, I had moved back to Virginia, but I seriously considered taking a special trip back there just to confront them about the rumor, because the bus driver had a wife and children and rumors like that could be so harmful. Especially if they were untrue.

You know how you hear so many sermons in church, but some are so good and teach such a good lesson that they stick with you? Well, I specifically remembered the pastor there talking to us about spreading rumors. He used the example of someone having a pillow stuffed with feathers and somehow the pillow tearing and the feathers blowing away. When the person tried to collect the feathers, he couldn't, because the wind had taken them to too many different places. I felt as though the people in the church should've known better. "Church" people can be some of the most heartless and thoughtless people sometimes, and anyone who's had any dealings with them knows that I'm not just saying this just to be saying it, but because it's true.

I wonder if they ever found out that the real man I was dating, John, was the pastor's very own first cousin. . . .

Although I had a lot of mixed feelings about this church, it will always be very special to me, because it was there that Michael and Michelle were baptized. I can still remember the anxiety I felt when the date of the next baptizing service was announced and the twins told me that they wanted to do it. I stayed up half the night before the service talking to them about it, making sure that they knew exactly what it meant and the importance of it. Although I was only ten when I left the church in Ohio, I could still remember the strictness of the pastor there as well as the not so strict but just as serious pastor in Virginia when it came to things like baptisms and taking Holy Communion. I knew that if Michael and Michelle did not know the seriousness of these things and I let them do it anyway, simply because they wanted to, I would be the one who would have to answer for it, not them. Anyway, after I was satisfied that the twins understood and sent them to bed, I still stayed up for the rest of the night entertaining the emotion line. I wished so bad that my mom was there with me.

The next day my stomach was in knots. They looked so tiny standing in the middle of the pool with the pastor. Michael was first.

"I baptize you in the name of the Father, of the Son, and of the Holy Ghost."

Michelle was next.

"I baptize you in the name of the Father, of the Son, and of the Holy Ghost."

I held my breath as they both went under the water. When they came up, they both seemed to be glowing. I couldn't concentrate on the rest of the service for thinking about my twins. I loved them so much, I think I would've died for them right then if I had to. . . .

I enjoyed my job and my church equally, which is hard for a lot of people to do. I always made myself have fun everywhere I ever worked, because, like I said, it made the day go by much easier. Up to this point in my life, though, this job had the funniest people whom I had ever worked with.

There were only about ten of us who actually worked together, so I guess having less people to deal with made things a little easier too. The supervisor was a trip. He was in a wheelchair, and he was always either jolly or mean. He didn't bother you too much if you showed him that you could be just as mean as him, though, as I had to do a *few* times.

His wife, daughter, and son also worked there. They were all good people and I liked them a lot. Even though the daughter was a lot younger than I was, we still bonded, and we confided in each other a lot. Once we even went to the mall in a nearby town together. Another time we exercised together. The son was the typical good-looking white boy. You know, the tall blond with blue eyes type. He wanted to be a rapper. Once he did a rap for me that he'd made up, and it was pretty good, if I say so myself.

The real "trip" family, though, was the owner, his wife, and their son and daughter. The owner made everybody "jump" and appear busy when he came around, but after I talked to him, I found out that he was just as crazy as the rest of us. The wife used to make us all laugh about how crazy she was for her dog. The daughter reminded me a lot of Bette Midler, with her personality and the way she wore her hair, and the thing about it was that she actually was pursuing a singing career. She let me hear a tape of her group once and they were pretty good. The son was in college, and get this—he was currently going to William & Mary, the very same college that James had graduated from.

After two years, I had had enough and was ready to move back home. I have two favorite memories about living in New York. One was when a traveling

production company came to town and had an audition for children at the community theater for
the play *Pinocchio*.

I saw the audition announcement in the newspaper and took the twins. When we got there and saw
how many other children had come (about 600,
the newspaper later said), Michelle automatically
chickened out. We sat in the audience and watched
as Michael made cut after cut. They were cutting
children so fast it was scary. Children were crying
because their feelings were hurt, mommas were
fussing because they thought that the audition was
biased, and Michael was steady, hanging in there.

Once when the director had them say their name
and age with as much "feeling" as they could, Michael
yelled out, "Michael Williams! Age eight!" Michelle and I were cracking up, because she and Michael
had just had a birthday and Michael must've been
so nervous that he forgot. When he realized the mistake he'd made, he made a funny face. He made the
cut, and then they had to do it again. When it was
Michael's turn, he yelled out, "Michael Williams! Age
nine!" When he looked out in the audience at us, I
made the motion of cutting my throat. Michelle was
cracking up. He shook his head and started laughing
as if to say he knew he had messed up as well. That
was the last cut. Michael made it.

When he came into the audience, where we were,
to tell us the part he had, he said he was in the
"crew." We started laughing because we thought that
meant he was going to be working the curtains and
stuff like that, but it wasn't. He was one of the little
"bad kids" who tried to make Pinocchio skip school.

The rehearsals were long and hard. Michael came

home during rehearsal breaks, because we lived right around the corner from the theater. He was so tired. During the very last rehearsal, Michelle and I laughed at him so hard when he came home for lunch because he had on stage make-up. His lips were painted red and he had rouge on his cheeks. He looked so cute.

The night of the play, I was so proud of him. It also made me feel good that the pastor of our church and his wife came. They said they could hear me yelling over everyone else at the end of the play when they introduced the actors and called out Michael's name.

My other favorite memory was when my family came to visit me for Christmas. It was Mom, Liz and her son, Eugene, Clarita, and Alvin. We had a ball.

Of course, Liz sang a solo at my church and I was so proud of her. She sung a song that we all love to hear her sing called "I Must Go On." When she was called up, everyone was so full of curiosity and anticipation that you could actually feel it in the air. When Liz started to sing, I closed my eyes and kept them closed during the whole song so that I wouldn't see or hear anything else but her voice. I hadn't realized how much I'd missed it. When she finished, she got a standing ovation, just as I expected.

Besides the performance at our church, that year the kids from our church did the Christmas play at the Boys Club and at one of the local elementary schools. Michael and Michelle were in the play and Mom thought it was so cute that she went to see it all three times.

The part of their visit that we all enjoyed the most was when we did our last-minute Christmas shopping.

Everybody was packed in one car and it reminded me of when a whole lot of circus clowns pack inside a little Volkswagen. The thing about it was that we were going to the same mall in the nearby city that I had gone to with my supervisor's daughter, and that I had been to a few other times with other people, but now that I was going with my family, I just couldn't remember the way.

"This is the wrong way again. Make a U-turn here and go back from whence thy came," I kept saying. Everybody was cracking up. After we got back to my apartment and unloaded the car, we all got ready to go to church again.

The New Year's Eve service at the church was so beautiful. Never before and never since have I been in a church service where the sanctuary was filled with so much love. I wondered why it couldn't be that way all the time. . . .

Chapter 26

I was excited to be going back home. My brother, Jr., and Clarita's husband, Alvin, came to get me in a rented truck. Talk about a countryman, Alvin came all the way there with no shoes! I don't mean with no shoes *on* now, I mean *no shoes!*

I was so happy when I got back home. I came to the conclusion that I loved to travel, but I could never make myself happy living somewhere else. It hadn't happened up to that point, anyway.

When we first came back home, the twins had to go through the accent trauma all over again, because now they had a northern accent and we were in the South again. What in the world is the big deal about having a different accent? I guess the way people talk is the very first way to tell that they're "different." Nevertheless, they were happy to be back home too.

I came back just in time to register Michael for the Little League football team at the neighborhood recreation center. I went to the first couple of practices with him, but I had to stop, because I couldn't stand the way Michael was being thrown around like he was. The first time it happened, I looked at him and he looked back at me with a look of sadness in his eyes that I couldn't stand.

"Do you want to go home?" I mouthed to him, so no one else could hear me. He shook his head no.

On top of that, his coach seemed to be unnecessarily hard on him. Later the coach told me that the reason he was so hard on Michael was that although Michael was big for his age, he was too soft and had to toughen up if he was going to keep playing. What made it so bad was that the boys' weight and not their age determined what team they played on, so Michael was put with the bigger boys who had previously played. Nevertheless, I couldn't stand to watch the practices, so Michelle and I would go around the corner to watch the cheerleaders practice while we waited for Michael.

At Michael's first game, it seemed like he wasn't going to play. James's father and stepmom were there to see him too. Michael looked so cute in his uniform but pitiful at the same time, because he was riding the bench.

"Look who they putting in the game!" James's father yelled in the last quarter of the game as Michael ran onto the field. You would think that after all the football games I had been to in my life up to this point, I would understand what Michael did when he went on the field, but I didn't. All I know is that I was clapping and yelling like crazy and whatever he did must've been good, because ever since then he played in all the team's other games (the whole game through).

That next year Michelle was a Little League

cheerleader. She was good, because she had watched the cheerleaders practice the previous year and knew all the cheers already. From the age of two, Michelle had been a very good dancer, so the moves were second nature for her. She looked so cute in her uniform. The cheering coaches were perfectionists. You know the type—used to be cheerleaders in high school and just couldn't let go. They used to be so mean to the girls during practice, making them repeat cheers over and over or make them run the track when they messed up on a cheer. However, when the girls cheered at the games, their hard practice really showed. They always put on an awesome halftime show.

One day around this same time, Mom called me when she had come from the mall. She was so excited. She told me that she went to JCPenney (her favorite store in the whole wide world) and saw Wayne, my friend from high school. Mom was almost as excited as I was, because she knew how much I loved Wayne.

As soon as Mom gave me his number and we hung up, I called Wayne. I was so happy to get in contact with him again. We couldn't wait to get together as we made bets on which of us had been "through" the most since we had last talked. I couldn't imagine him possibly going through a lot of drama, because he was such a no-nonsense person. Then I thought about the unexpected turns I had to make in my own life, and the fact that nothing was impossible. Sure enough, Wayne had been in the service, had gotten married, had had a little girl, had gotten divorced, had gained custody of his daughter *and* stepson, and had gotten out of the army because his sister Betty (the one who raised him) was dying of cancer and he wanted to be close to her. That was just like Wayne.

Wayne and I became inseparable. Whenever a new movie came out, we would go on the first night it showed, and it seemed like there wasn't a restaurant in the city that we hadn't tried at least once, especially the buffets. I didn't even have to worry about feeling guilty about leaving the twins, because we took them with us too. Mom knew that I loved Wayne like a brother and she eventually started calling him her son.

I also automatically got involved in my old church as soon as I came back home. I was so glad to be back with the church and the members were glad to see me. Most of them anyway. Of course, I got involved in working with the young people, which included directing the youth choir, as well as introducing some of the ideas I brought back with me from the church up north, like the praise dancing, a praise and worship team, and different children's plays.

I was a faithful church member and hard worker, which is why I don't understand why it was that when I fell behind on my bills and went to the church for financial help, the members there treated me like they did. The church's trustee board actually drew up a contract that stipulated the terms on which I was supposed to pay the money back. After I signed it, I talked to several people who said that it was actually against the law for them to do that, because the church wasn't a lending institution. It really didn't matter to me at the time. All I know is that I was behind on my bills and was trying hard to hold on to the house that I was renting at the time.

It was the first house the children had ever lived

in and they loved it so much. We had a backyard with a garage, where I put a basketball hoop on the door. The twins had a ball when all the kids in the neighborhood would come over to play.

I also did something that I never thought I'd do. I got Michael a dog. We read in the classified ads where someone was giving puppies away. The dog was so cute. I forgot what we named him, but he was a black Lab mixed with something else and Michael really loved that dog.

Once when Michael went to the store for me, he took the dog with him, and while he was in the store, someone stole the dog. I immediately knew something was wrong when I saw Michael coming around the corner stomping his feet and crying.

About a week later, someone in the neighborhood was giving away pit bull puppies and Michael came home with one. I didn't want a pit bull, because of the horrible stories I had heard of how vicious they grew up to be, but this puppy was so cute and helpless that I gave in.

All of us fell in love with the dog, even Michelle, and this was very surprising because just like me when I was younger, Michelle had a natural fear of dogs. About two weeks after we had him, someone stole him too.

"Why people got to steal? Why they don't just look in the paper and get one like we did?" Michael asked me as he cried so pitifully.

Eventually I decided to leave my church because besides the trustee board being so mean about the money that I "borrowed" from them, there were really some hateful people there and I just couldn't take it anymore. (Oh, and by the way, I still lost the house, because I just couldn't afford the rent with the kind of job that I had.)

Anyway, you know how in every church there's one family who knows everything, feels like they have to be in charge of everything, and will hurt anybody and everybody's feelings to do it? Well, there was one in our church too, and I felt like their hatred and jealousy was so strong, it had started to affect the whole church. I could no longer stand it. The sad part about it was that everyone in the church knew how this family was, but no one seemed to be able to do anything about it, including the pastor, Bishop Edison.

Once, the head of this family disagreed with me about the time I decided to put on the children's Christmas play and we ended up in Bishop Edison's office. When it looked like Bishop Edison was going to let me have the play at the time I wanted, the head of the family bust out with a question that had nothing to do with Christmas.

"And by the way, when are you gonna pay back the money we loaned you?" I shot her a look but didn't answer. Bishop Edison was cool about it and said we would talk about the money later because we were in his office to discuss the play.

"Just keep things the way they are," Bishop Edison said, "and remember that if you don't have Christmas in your hearts, it doesn't matter what else you do." He was so cool. After the meeting, though, he held me behind.

"You really do need to try hard to pay back some more of the money, Ivy, because while it don't make that much difference to me, the trustee board, who is in charge of the church's money, is fussing about it." Of course, the trustee board was made up of "the family."

I couldn't take it anymore. It had started to directly affect my spiritual growth. My mother wasn't too pleased with my decision to leave the church, because we had been there for so long.

"The Lord got you there for those children, Ivy, and you shouldn't let nobody keep you from doing that." Although I agreed with Mom, I just didn't know where to draw the line between doing what the Lord had me there to do, and being so discouraged or having to fight so hard whenever I did it. I was in church long enough to know that if your heart wasn't in the right place when you did something for God, you might as well not even bother. Evidently everybody didn't know this. I had to get out of there. . . .

Long after I left the church, I got a letter from the trustees about the money I owed. By that time, I decided I wasn't going to pay back the money, because they were being so nasty about it, and besides, it had been so long ago since I'd borrowed it. I told Johnice about it and showed the letter to her while she was doing my hair.

"Dag, Ivy, that don't make no sense!" she said. "I wouldn't pay them nothing, and if they tried to take it any further, I'd put it in the newspaper!" She felt the same way about it as I did. How in the world could the trustees of a church be that hung up on such a small amount of money that they helped out one of their own members with? A single parent at that? Especially a *tithe-paying* member who took part in as many different ministries of the church as I did? It's not that I expected them to pay me for anything that I did; I just felt that it was mean of them to harass me like they were.

Mom said that the main thing about it was that I did *agree* to pay it back and that's what they were looking at. Deep in my heart, I knew it was right to pay the money back, because I had agreed to do so, but I think the people who were after me to pay the money back and the way they were going about it made my heart harden. (I'm pretty sure you remember who "they" were. But what "they" didn't know was that I had found out that a member of "their" immediate family had stolen a large amount of money from the church once, and that nothing had ever been said about it. Nothing. Ever.) It meant a lot to Mom that I paid the money back, though, because by this time she was one of the mothers of the church. Later I found out that Mom had felt so bad about the loan that *she* had started to pay on it. Only to keep them from getting the rest of it from my Mom, which, by the way, I felt was real low, I decided to go ahead and pay it back. Church people can be the worst people sometimes. They really can.

After my return home, I also endured two very sad times for my family. My mom started having a lot of pain in her lower stomach area. When she went to the doctor several times they discovered that she had cancer of the uterus. She had an operation and to God be the glory, it was successful.

While my mom was recuperating over at my Aunt May's house, though, Clarita called to say that someone had stabbed Alvin in his heart. He was not as fortunate. He died that same night. . . .

Wayne was the perfect friend. I couldn't have made it without him by my side.

Chapter 27

Michael and Michelle did well in school and a lot of times were chosen for special things. While in the fifth grade, they were chosen for the all-city elementary school choir. I wasn't surprised, because of the way they had learned to sing while we'd lived up north. The concert was held at the intermediate school that I went to. When I walked in the school, the memories of when I went there came back so strong that I really had to *make* myself concentrate on the children's concert. It was good and I was so proud of them. They were really special kids. I'm not saying this because they were my kids, but because it's true.

In the sixth grade, the twins decided to join the band. Michelle played the clarinet and Michael played the baritone saxophone. The band director asked me if could Michael change to playing the tuba, because the band was short on tuba players and Michael "picked up" so well. I automatically thought about myself when I was in elementary school—how I changed instruments every year. Besides the Autoharp, I also played the violin, and then the clarinet.

While they were in the band, I used to embarrass the twins so bad. At their concerts, I would wait until everybody else finished applauding, and then when it was completely quiet, I would holler, "Michael and Michelle Williams!" Michael would bust out in this big grin, but Michelle would drop and shake her head like she was thinking, *Lord have mercy, why don't that woman be quiet?*

By the time the twins reached the eighth grade, Michael would take part in a lot of extra things, but not Michelle. Michael was always more of a "people person" than Michelle. When it came to people and choosing friends, Michelle was a lot like her Aunt Liz. She just didn't like a lot of stupid stuff or phony people and could spot them a mile away, even at that young age. Sometimes it bothered her that she didn't have a lot of friends like Michael did, but when she added up the cost, she decided she'd really rather not be bothered.

Michael, on the other hand, was more of an outgoing person. Although he was only in the eighth grade, he played football for the high school team, and because he was the only one, his coach called him "eighth grader."

Around this time, much to my family's and closest friend's disapproval, I had pretty much given up on James giving me any kind of financial help with the twins. After all, it had been about five years since he had sent them anything. Not even as much as a fifty-cent birthday card. I knew that wherever James was, he still loved the twins, and every so often when they visited their grandfather's house, they would come back home and tell me that they had talked to their dad on the phone. I just couldn't understand why he hadn't tried to see them in all that time or send them something every once in a while—a letter, a card, *something*. The twins had everything that they needed. Their grandfather and I made sure of that. But like I said, I had given up on James's help. I got tired of trying to chase him down. I thought it was a shame, though.

One day Michelle got real sick. She said she felt weak and she couldn't keep any food down. I thought it was no more than a twenty-four-hour bug that was going around, so I gave her Tylenol and orange juice, but she threw that up too. The next two days, when she didn't get any better, I took her to the emergency room. She took a shower before she left but could hardly stand in the shower. I was getting scared. When the emergency room doctor took X-rays, he said her lungs were black with pneumonia and it was good that I had brought her in when I did. She had to stay in the hospital. I had no idea how I would pay the hospital bill by myself, so I applied for Medicaid. Social Services wanted to know her father's information. Child support was back in the picture.

My caseworker told me that when they finally contacted James, the first question he asked her was, "How did you find find me?"

"That's my job," she answered. "What I need to know from you is your intentions in helping to take care of your children." She said that James acted real ugly the whole time they spoke.

"Well, I'm in school and can barely take care of myself," James spat back at her.

"I understand that, but the children still have to be taken care of," the caseworker said.

"Well I just don't have no money," James repeated until they ended the conversation.

I started to spend so much time at the child support office that the caseworker and I built a personal relationship. Her name was Gladys Salano, and she, just like I, couldn't figure out why everybody else understood that the children were James's responsibility except James. She finally left the job, but before she did, we had a long talk.

"Make sure you stay on this, Ivy, because James is fighting this thing so hard that I'm afraid it'll eventually fall by the wayside," was one of the last things she said to me. I guess she had worked with the agency so long that she had seen it happen before and didn't want it to happen to me.

"Oh, I will, Ms. Salano. I *promise* I will." It was one promise I intended to keep, no matter what the emotional or financial cost. . . .

Chapter 28

My family got together and rented a van to visit my father back in Ohio, who had lung cancer and was in a nursing home. I didn't want to go because my money "wasn't right." My brother tried hard to convince me to go.

"Come on, Ivy. You don't need no money, because the van's already paid for and we can just bunk in the hotel room together."

Even the twins told me that I should go and that they would stay with James's father to save money, but still I couldn't be convinced.

They left that Friday after everybody got off work. I know they had a good time, because we really loved to travel as a family, stopping to eat and playing games along the way. Once when we went back to Cleveland for an appreciation service our old church had for my Aunt Mary, we had a ball. That was the first time that Liz, Clarita, and I sung a song in church together. The church members enjoyed it, but not half as much as I did. Then, during the service when we all got to say something, I had them cracking up about how one of the ladies named Sister Gibbs, who was an usher when I was little, was *still* an usher and *still* snatching folks' children around. Even Sister Gibbs was cracking up.

Anyway, they took a lot of pictures while they were there visiting my father and showed them to me when they came back. That was on the Sunday that they returned. I promised myself I would go the next time.

That Tuesday morning, Clarita called me at work to tell me that my father was dead. . . .

When we rented another van to go back to Ohio that very next weekend to bury my father, I wouldn't talk to anybody all the way there. I was angry with all of them. I felt that they were all being phony about their feelings about my father. You see, I was my father's favorite. This was not because he loved me any more than his other children, but because of the time we spent together. (Remember, while Dad and I spent time on the porch together, my brother was away in the military, Liz was with her friends, and Clarita was a little baby.) Also, my mother, even until this day, always talked about the many ways in which my father mistreated her while they were together, and I felt that she should have forgiven him for it and let it go. (I know I'm being hypocritical when I'm having such a hard time letting go of the house party beating my Mom gave me, but it seems easier when you judge someone else in his or her wrongdoing. Much easier.)

At the funeral when the army men presented my mom with my dad's flag, she wouldn't touch it. She nodded her head toward us (her children) as the army man had a confused look on his face. Somehow

I ended up with it. Liz said that she thought my brother should have it, but there was no way that I was going to part with that flag. No way.

Later I realized that it wasn't my family whom I was angry with, but myself. Till this day I haven't been able to forgive myself for not going with the rest of my family to see my father for the very last time. . . .

Chapter 29

The year was 1995 and I was thirty-seven years old. By this time, I had pretty much given up on men. Not altogether, but just enough not to let them come before what I was supposed to be doing as far as making my *own* life a better one. I figured if I wasn't already into a career by then, I certainly should be working on it, and up to that point, the men in my life had only distracted instead of encouraged me. I had been feeling this way longer than I'd realized, because I hadn't dated since 1992. I could fake it no longer—I was lonely. Wayne and I were still hanging tight and you barely saw one of us without the other, but it wasn't the same.

Christmas had just passed and so had New Year's—the two holidays to spend with the one you love. February's Valentine's Day was quickly approaching, with my birthday close behind it in March, and I really wanted to spend them with someone special.

Each morning, a particular young man stopped by my job on his way to work. Every time he caught my eye, he would nod his head to say hello and give

me a real nice smile. One day he gave another girl
who worked there his phone number to give to me.
I thought if he was going to be the next one I went
out with, I should go ahead and give him a call so
that we could at least talk on the phone a couple of
times first. The first question I asked him, of course,
was if he was married and he said no. After a few
more phone calls, I invited him over, and after a few
more visits, he was my "new man." He and Michael
hit it off right away, but Michelle wasn't so sure. . . .

Terrell said the reason he found me so different
was that I didn't always have my hand out like the
other women he'd dated, although he still insisted
on helping me financially. As a matter of fact, Terrell soon started to pay *all* my bills, but I just never
asked him for money, because from the time I was
grown, I felt that to *automatically* expect money
from a man just because you were "going" with him
was a form of prostitution. I had a girlfriend who
disagreed with me very strongly on this.

"Girl, please, that ain't prostitution—that's *sur-
vival*," she'd say. We used to fuss about it back and
forth, both of us refusing to give in.

Anyway, I could tell that this was the type of
woman whom Terrell had dealt with in the past, because every Thursday when he got paid, like clock-
work, he'd ask me what I needed. I'd actually be
tongue-tied, because I'd never had anyone take
care of me like that before. When I'd tell him that
I was okay, he'd insist until I gave in and took whatever he offered me.

My and Terrell's favorite pastime was lying on the
floor listening to music while we sang along with the
tapes, especially when a song came on that a man

and woman sang together. Our favorite was "Back Together Again" by Roberta Flack and Donny Hathaway. We just knew we were throwing down when we sang our own part, then laughed when it was the other person's turn.

"Nigga, please. I'm just *making* myself sound bad so I won't hurt yo' feelings," I used to say.

"Whatever. Gone now and finish yo' part and stop stalling," he'd answer.

Even when he wasn't there, I used to play songs that reminded me of him and even made him a tape of the songs so that he could listen to them while we were apart. Once when I was listening to the radio when we'd first started dating, someone was singing about how he'd finally found "someone to love, someone to touch, someone to hold, and someone to know." Till this day, that song reminds me of Terrell. It's so amazing how a song can be so perfect for the way you feel at that moment about someone, that regardless of what you go through in the future with that same person, hearing the song can make you remember your first feelings for that person so vividly.

We also spent a lot of time at the mall and different eating places. Every time I turned around, he was buying me gifts of diamonds, gold, or both. Mom said I was starting to look like Mr. T. Terrell was really good to me. If the twins and I weren't out with Wayne, we were out with Terrell. I felt like I had the best of both worlds.

Everyone who knew about my previous relationships was happy for me: Wayne, Lydia and her sister, and Gloria. They said that it looked like I had finally found Mr. Right. I thought so too.

During that time, the new church that I had

started to attend had a television ministry. It came on every Sunday morning, and right before the pastor gave his message, he had one of the soloists in the church sing a selection. Once he asked me to do a solo.

I was nervous about actually singing on television, but it didn't take me long to decide on what I was going to sing. It was my favorite song, because by this time I'd finally realized that the words of a song were so much more important than how the song sounded. The name of the song was "He'll Find a Way" and the chorus went:

> *"For I know that if He can paint a sunset,*
> *put the stars in space,*
> *and if He can raise up mountains,*
> *and calm storm-tossed waves,*
> *and if He can conquer death forever,*
> *and open Heaven's gates,*
> *then I know for you, He'll find a way."*

I really loved that song, because it let me know that my problems were nothing for God if He had created the whole universe. It was so true and encouraging and I tried to hold on to that thought so many times, even though most of the time I failed. . . .

A couple of days after the program, I got a call from Terrell's mom. She told me that when she saw me on TV and heard me singing like that, she couldn't keep hiding the truth about Terrell from me. *Uh-oh, I knew it was too good to be true,* I thought.

She told me that Terrell was using drugs and had been for some time, that he had taken some things from her like her VCR and a sterling silver tea set and sold them, and that he had given her money a few times but then took it back. When she told me that, I thought about how he had come back for money he had given me a few times too, but I hadn't paid it any mind, because he always gave it back "with interest" just like he said he would.

After my conversation with Terrell's mom, I started to think about the different places where the children and I had lived. All of them (except the house) had been in low-income places where most of the women were on some kind of government assistance. I didn't think that anything was wrong with needing government assistance, because some of the time I did too. It's just that these women also had a lot of different men in and out of their and their children's lives. Most of these men were alcoholics, drug users, or both, and I thought it was a shame how the women took what the government gave them to support them and their children and instead, used it to support the habits of these men. I used to watch them all outside arguing, fussing, and fighting all the time, but they still held on to the men. I felt that these women were putting these men before their children and I vowed never to do that. Never. The peace that I had in my home with the twins meant so much more to me than having that kind of man. Than having *any* kind of man.

I also felt that the example I had set for the twins up to that point had paid off. Right then we lived in a project that was so bad that it had its own police station. "Excuse me, miss," one of the officers called to me one day.

"Yes?"

"I wanted to say something to you about your

children." I immediately started wondering what
kind of trouble the twins had gotten into and why
they felt that they couldn't tell me.

"Yes?" I repeated.

"I just wanted to tell you that you have the most
respectful children out here."

"Thanks. . . ." I was so proud of them.

Also, there was a 7-Eleven in the neighborhood
that was bought by some foreigners. "I know your
children. They the only children not try to steal
from me," one of the foreigners told me one day.

I'll never forget the feeling I got from these men
telling me this. I'm not saying that my children
were perfect, by any means. I'm just saying that the
values and morals that I worked so hard to instill in
them were showing and for that I was grateful.

After much thought, I called Terrell and told
him that if he chose to live that kind of life it was his
business, but I couldn't let him drag me and the
twins into it. He said that he understood and we
broke up, but he still called every day and I missed
him a lot. A whole lot . . .

One Sunday morning, Terrell called me.

"Hey, what you doing?"

"Getting ready for church."

"Can I go?"

"I guess so. . . ." I knew Terrell was only trying to
use this as an excuse to be with me that day, but
how could I tell anyone that he or she couldn't go
to church?

That Sunday, the preacher preached about God's
love, as he often did. I liked the way he preached, because it seemed that so many preachers' sermons
were about "Heaven or Hell" or "the wages of sin . . .

but the gift of God." I'm not saying that anything is wrong with these types of sermons. As a matter of fact, I wouldn't say that anything is wrong with *any* type of sermon, because I know that sermons are supposed to be messages from God. But I feel that the average Christian already knew these things and what we really needed to know was how to deal with day-to-day issues *after* we became Christians. This preacher often preached about God's unconditional love. He made sure that we clearly understood that regardless of what we did—or still may be doing—God still loved us unconditionally, and the way he preached these sermons made you think that if God indeed loved us that strongly, it was almost impossible not to love Him back and feel that we owe Him our very lives.

I'm a firm believer that it doesn't matter why a person *thinks* he or she came to church; it was intended for that person to be there. This was definitely the case with Terrell being in church on that Sunday, because when the preacher got finished preaching and made the altar call, Terrell gave his life to Christ. He said he wanted to change and I believe he meant it. We got back together and I thought he was the perfect man for me. Lots of times we hear people use the phrase (and sometimes use it ourselves) "where have you been all my life," but I *really* felt that way when it came to Terrell.

Terrell was a hard worker and although he didn't make a whole lot of money, with what he did make, he did well. Real well. He said he didn't want me on the public system, so we made plans and worked hard *together* so that I could get off of it. I totally trusted Terrell. He gave me no reason not to.

Lots of times on Sundays after church we all would

go out for dinner and then ride around to different newly developed communities or different car lots to look at homes and cars that we wanted and vowed to own someday.

"I think we got a shot at it," Terrell would say.

"We shol do—a shot in our hindpot if we don't get off these people's property," Michael would answer. That boy ain't have no sense. Michelle would scream in laughter as we drove off.

My friendship with Wayne was still going strong. Every year, he took me out for my birthday, but then I'd have to fuss him out, because when it was his birthday, I could never return the treat, because he could never be found. The year was 1996, and again we made plans to go out for my birthday, but, for some reason, he came by a few days earlier. When he got to my place, I was on the phone with a girl-friend whom I'd previously worked with but had not talked to since I'd left the job. I was so happy to hear from the girl that I loudly chattered on while Wayne waited for me to get off the phone. He eventually grew tired of waiting, stood up, and said he'd see me later. I smiled at him and waved. I knew that the next time I saw him, he was going to give me the business for keeping him waiting like I did.

When my birthday came, Wayne didn't show up.

Chapter 30

About two weeks after my birthday, Mildred called me. She worked at the same place as Wayne and asked me when was the last time I had heard from him.

"About a couple of weeks ago, girl. You know it was my birthday and he always takes me out, but this time that nigger didn't even show! He *know* he gon git cussed out when I lay eyes on him again!"

Silence.

"Ivy."

"What?"

"I heard he was found dead in his condo."

"That's not true. I just saw him. Hang up. I'm calling his niece. I'll call you back later."

My hands were shaking as I looked up Joey's number. Her husband answered the phone.

"Hello."

"Mike?"

"Yeah."

"This is Ivy. Please tell me where Wayne is."

Silence.

"Mike?"

"We found him dead in his condo last week."

More silence. I still refused to believe it.

"Let me speak to Joey."

Joey told me the whole story of how they thought it was odd that no one had heard from Wayne in a few days, and when they went to his condo, his car was there but he didn't answer his door. She went on to tell me of how they put pinecones behind the wheels of his car tires to see if the car was being moved, and when they came back, the pinecones were still there. She finally got to the part of how they eventually got someone to unlock the door to his condo, and they found him dead inside. My friend. My brother. Dead. As she talked I felt myself growing weaker. . . .

When we hung up, I looked ahead with a blank stare. Everything in the room started to look blurry as my eyes filled with tears. Terrell, who was beside me during the phone call, finally spoke.

"You okay?"

In my mind, I started to scream at him.

No, I'm not okay! This was my very dearest friend in the whole wide world! I loved him like a brother and could talk to him about anything! Anything! We laughed and cried together! We shared secrets with each other that we knew we couldn't share with anyone else! We talked about our children and what we wanted for them! We talked about the mistakes we made in our past relationships and how things would be different the next time! I knew I could count on him for any kind of help, whether it was financial or emotional, when I could count on no one else! No one! I . . .

"Ivy?"

"Yeah, I'm okay." I went upstairs and went to bed, praying that when I woke, it would have all been just a bad dream. . . .

Chapter 31

Wayne's death put me in a serious mood of depression and I felt that if anyone could understand why, it should've been Terrell. We argued because we planned on being married on the very same day as Wayne's funeral. He said he didn't see why we should change our plans, and I couldn't believe how insensitive he was being. I went to talk to Elaine, Wayne's sister, and she told me that Wayne would've wanted me to go ahead with my plans, because my happiness was so important to him. I disagreed, but she said that if I married Terrell on that day I would always remember a happy occasion instead of just a sad one, and again, she knew that that's what Wayne would've wanted for me.

I finally gave in and then I sadly waited for the funeral of my best friend. A few days before the funeral, I was listening to a cassette tape that Wayne had loaned me wondering how long I was going to be depressed and hurting the way that I was. Just at the right moment, Anita Baker started to sing "Only for a While." The timing was so perfect that it was almost as if Wayne himself was answering me. I looked at the tape player and, through my tears, mustered up a smile.

I was on the program at Wayne's funeral. As I walked closer to the front of the church and to Wayne's casket, I felt my legs getting weak. When I finally stood behind the podium, I looked in the section where the family was seated until I found Elaine's face. She smiled and nodded at me to give me the encouragement that she knew I desperately needed. I started to softly speak.

"In life, we come across a lot of people, but very few that we can really call a friend. . . ."

I told them about the kind of friend that Wayne was to me and how that made me love him the way that I did. Then I referred to Ecclesiastes 3 in the Bible, where it talks about "time."

"When I heard about Wayne's death, I felt that the time was not right, because although we had done so much together, there was so much more that we still had planned. . . ."

My mind quickly flashed back to the many conversations we'd had, like the one about seeing our children graduate from high school and college and then making them treat us to a vacation that we knew we would desperately need by that time. Other times we talked about our grandchildren and how we hoped that our children would set better examples for them, especially when it came to things like taking our education seriously and keeping good credit.

". . . Nevertheless, because the Bible tells us that there's a time for everything, I knew it was time for Wayne to die, and I'm really going to miss him, because in life, we come across a lot of people, but very few that we can really call a friend."

Immediately after the funeral, Terrell and I were married.

Chapter 32

I couldn't ask for a better husband. I looked forward to Terrell coming home from work every night so that we all could have dinner and then spend time together as a family; because it was the first time I had ever done that on a daily basis, it was really priceless. Usually after dinner, we would clear the table and play cards or a board game. Guesstures was our favorite. Terrell had even started to make progress with breaking down the wall that Michelle had built between them.

One day, Michael and Michelle brought home Upward Bound applications from school. This was a program where the high school children stayed on a college campus during the summer, and went to classes in preparation for when they became college students themselves. I anxiously signed them, thinking about the time that I had had while I was in the same program and hoping that Michael and Michelle would share the same experience. What I was mostly excited about, though, was the time that I'd have alone with Terrell while they were gone.

Terrell held true to his promise to leave the drugs alone, and even when he smoked a cigarette, he went out on the porch. I knew that the sudden change in his lifestyle was hard on him and I tried to keep him company as much as I could, but often I'd fall asleep before he did and he hated it.

One morning right before Terrell was getting ready to leave for work, he told me that he wasn't coming straight home. I knew exactly how frustrated and bored he had become with my going to sleep on him all the time, and I instantly became afraid of what he was about to do to otherwise entertain himself.

I started to cry.

"You have to."

"Why?"

"Because we're having a baby."

I heard the truck horn blow for him. Although it was right in front of the house, it sounded so far away.

"Who's having a baby?"

"We are."

He smiled at me and wiped my tears.

"Don't cry. We'll talk when I come home."

I had a lot of mixed feelings about having a baby at such an old age; after all, I was then thirty-eight and the twins were fifteen. Michelle felt pretty much the same as I did. Like myself, Michelle cared more about how she felt at the moment.

Michael, on the other hand, came from a totally different angle. He wanted to know if we could *afford* a baby. You see, I always included the children in my financial decisions. Lots of people don't agree with this. Terrell was one of those people.

"Why do you tell your kids so much of your business," he once asked me. I explained to him that I felt (and still do) that every single mother with a low income should include her children in family financial discussions for two reasons. The first reason is that if the children know exactly how much the mother makes and what *has* to be done with it, they'll know what's left over for other things. The children will quickly learn the difference between "wants" and "needs" and will know that if there's something they merely *want* and the mother says no, she's not saying it just to be saying it. She's saying it because she knows that the children's *needs* must be met first. The second reason is that if the children see their mother "juggling" the bills and having to struggle so hard to make ends meet, it will hopefully make the daughter more determined not to become a single mother before she completes her education and gets a good job, and make the son think twice about becoming a single father and leaving his girlfriend by herself to "juggle and struggle." Of course, the maturity of the children has to be at a certain level to understand these things, and to God be the glory, my twins were very mature.

I'll never forget the situation that had caused me to start thinking this way. I had taken the twins to Payless to shop for shoes. They were about five years old, but even at that young age, Michelle was never as picky as Michael when it came to fashion, name brands, and things like that. Anyway, Payless had a brand of tennis shoes called ProWings that I was buying for the twins at about that time. ProWings came in a lot of colors and styles. I had previously bought the twins a few pairs, because although they weren't name brand, they were still made well and outlasted the other tennis shoes in that store. Michelle quickly chose the kind she wanted, and then we began to walk around the store with Michael as he tried to decide. When he took too long, I chose a pair for him. When I told him to try them on, he wouldn't.

"Go 'head, Mike, and put the shoes on now. We gotta go. It's almost time for the bus and I'm tired. . . ."

"But I don't like those."

"Then what kind do you want? You already looked at every other pair they have."

"I don't like none of them."

Out of the corner of my eye, I could see a white woman glaring at us. I was losing my patience.

"Well, you have to pick *something*, Mike, and you can't choose something that's not here. Try these on now. . . ."

"But I don't like them kind."

"Put the shoes *on*, Michael!"

"I don't want those. . . ." He started to cry.

"What kind do you want, Mike?"

I don't know why I asked. I had a gut feeling of what he was going to say.

"I want some Reeboks."

I started to wonder what kind of tennis shoes his father, a captain in the army, wore. I was really beginning to hate him. . . .

Anyway, I was happy about my pregnancy, because I was totally in love with Terrell and would have done anything for him. Anything.

"You ain't lying—anybody old as *you* having a baby," my family and friends joked.

The twins left for Upward Bound that summer, and although I enjoyed the time alone with Terrell, it wasn't quite as "romantic" as I thought it would be. If I wasn't tired from the pregnancy, I was tired from running back and forth to the college for the twins.

Michael wanted to know if I could bring him some money, because all the guys were chipping in for pizza; Michelle needed sanitary pads; Michael needed swimming trunks; Michelle couldn't find her money and they were going to King's Dominion the next day, so she wanted to know if I could loan her some (I finally put her out of her misery by telling her that I'd put her money in her closet in one of her shoe boxes, because when I'd come to the campus earlier that day to bring the bar of soap that she'd requested, her door was unlocked and when I went to put the soap in her drawer, there was her money in plain view where anybody could've taken it); Michael forgot his basketball; somebody hurt Michelle's feelings, and when she called Michael's room to talk to him, she was hung up on, so she wanted to come home because I promised her that if she went and didn't like it she could; and this and that and that and this and hubba, hubba, hubba. . . .

All the running back and forth combined with the phone calls frustrated Terrell. He said I was doing nothing but spoiling the twins. He was right, but I had done it for so long that it was hard for me to stop.

On August 6, exactly one day before my due date, I went into labor. My pregnancy had gone well, but when I went to the hospital, my blood pressure was high and I wasn't dilating like I should've, so I ended up having another C-section. Everything turned out well. We had a precious baby girl. She weighted six pounds, nine ounces. I named her Terra, because she looked exactly like her dad.

When I got home from the hospital and went through the pile of mail, I found a child support check from James. It was my first one in eight years.

Chapter 33

The Christmas following Terra's birth, James came to see the twins. The line of emotions (remember them?) revisited me. Although I was upset at James for taking that long to see the twins, I was also proud of him, because he had indeed gone back to school and earned his master's *and* Ph.D. degrees. He was a professor at a very prestigious university. When I went to James's father's house to talk to James about how long he had been missing from the children's lives, I was shocked to see how he looked. He had gained over a hundred pounds and was almost bald on the top of his head. The hair that he did have left was mixed with gray, and his eyebrows also had some gray in them. It made me think about just how many years had gone by since I'd first met him in Patrice's room at Virginia State. After the initial greetings and small talk, I brought up the real reason I'd come to see him.

"James, please don't stay out of the children's lives like you did for the past eight years again, because . . ." He cut me off and told me that the way he stayed away from the twins was *my* fault and that he wasn't going to hear any "lectures" from me. At that point, I figured that it really didn't matter how much education he had, he would always be ignorant when it came to the importance of him being in his children's lives.

From then on, James kept in contact with the twins, but he and I could never have a decent conversation, especially when it came to child support. Every time that subject came up, he would say that it was my fault because of what I did to him when we were married. He still blames me to this day— some twenty-five years later. I imagine that I did hurt James, but I tried to explain to him that he wasn't supposed to make the children pay for what I did. I mean, did he actually think that the twins would accept that as an excuse for him not helping to take care of them or taking part in their lives as they were growing up? I guess it is true that although education and life experiences go hand in hand, they still are worlds apart. . . .

Chapter 34

The twins were growing up so fast. They had started working their first jobs, Michael at a fast-food restaurant and Michelle at a telemarketing center. Michael was still playing football and had practice after school. After football season, he'd trade the football uniform in for a wrestling uniform. His grades were still good, because he was naturally smart, but Michelle's good grades came as a result of her studying hard. They both were in the church choir. I finally went back to work after having Terra. Everybody had crazy schedules and we didn't spend as much time together as we used to, but we still had a lot of fun whenever we did.

We moved into a brick rancher. Although we were only renting, it still was my dream house and we had a lot of fun decorating it. The way we came across it was nothing short of a miracle.

I was unhappy with where we were living at the time, because someone had broken into our house, and besides, we needed something a little bigger than what we had. I'd started looking around in the "nicer" neighborhoods when I came across it. I stopped by the 7-Eleven, then decided to go home. Right around the corner from the 7-Eleven, I saw the house. There was a "for rent" sign in the yard and I pulled up in the yard and peeked in the window. The first thing to catch my eye was something I always wanted—a fireplace. The room looked so pretty with the plush carpet, fancy ceiling fan, and freshly painted walls. I left thinking it was no use—we would never be able to afford a place like that. Still, I couldn't get it out of my mind.

Michael was always missing the school bus, regardless of how much I fussed at him. I tried to give him the benefit of the doubt, because he did have a very busy schedule with football practice, his part-time job, and choir practices and all, but *every morning*? I told him that if he felt he was doing too many things, then he needed to make a choice of which was more important to him and let something else go. He continually promised that he would, but he never did.

After Michael missed the bus *again* one day, as I was driving him to school, I took him by the house to see what he thought. I knew he would be totally honest with his opinion, regardless of what I wanted to hear him say.

"It *is* nice, Ma, but I don't think we can afford something like this."

"Yeah, you probably right, son," I said. But I still couldn't stop thinking about the house. It was almost like something was telling me not to be afraid to ask about it, so I did.

When I called the number that was on the sign, some real estate office answering machine picked up. *Uh-oh*, I thought. I knew that real estate offices paid more attention to credit reports than personal owners, and ours wasn't too hot. I still left a message, but no one called me back.

That evening I took a chance and went to see it again. This time, I took Terrell with me and the door was open.

"Hey! Come on in," the man inside said.

"Hi," I said nervously. "We saw the sign in the yard and wanted to ask some questions. . . ."

"Well, it's my son's house, but you can look around while he's finishing some rewiring that he's working on in the basement."

The house was so pretty. It was totally remodeled and everything looked and smelled brand new. All of a sudden I started measuring each room with my feet.

"What you doing?" asked Terrell.

"Measuring the rooms. This is going to be our house—you'll see."

"You think so, huh?"

"I know so."

"Okay, when the man comes in here, I'ma let you talk." I loved Terrell's confidence in me.

The man who owned the house finally came in, apologized for taking so long, and shook our hands. I was nervous, but I looked him straight in the eyes while I talked to him.

"We're currently renting a house, but it's really too small and in a bad neighborhood. We want a bigger and nicer place. Our credit isn't that great, but we're in the process of clearing it up so that it won't keep stopping us from doing the things that we really want to do. . . ."

I thought he wasn't moved in the least by what I

was telling him, because he just gave me this blank stare. Then he gave me a piece of paper about the size of a matchbook and told me to write our name and number on it. I glanced over at the applications that were on the kitchen counter. The paper he gave me was so small I could hardly fit everything on there, but I put my and Terrell's names and our number on it and nervously handed it back to the man. As we left the house, we laughed and talked about the man like a dog, saying that at least he could've given us an application like he did the other people, even if he did think that it would probably be a waste of time. It was good that we had a sense of humor about it, even though we had the feeling that we had just been turned down. That's how we were. Anyway, we had pretty much given up on getting the house.

The next day, we got a phone call. A man asked for somebody who didn't live at our place. I told him that he had the wrong number, but I wasn't ready for him to hang up, because I had a feeling that I recognized his voice. It was the owner of the house. I didn't have to try too hard to keep him on the phone, though, because he wasn't ready to hang up either.

"I'm looking for a couple who came to look at my house yesterday," he said. I stared at Terrell, who was looking right back at me. I told the man that it was us.

"I was thinking about what you said," he continued, "and decided to give you a chance."

That night, I could barely sleep. I wanted to talk to Terrell, but I didn't want to wake him. I decided to whisper his name and if he answered, I'd know if he was asleep or not.

"Terrell."

"Huh?"

Good, he's awake.

"Do you realize what happened today?" Even though he was awake, I still continued to whisper.

"What you mean?"

"Do you remember all those applications that were on that kitchen counter in that house? They had all those people's information on them: their names, addresses, jobs, references—all that stuff. That little piece of paper we gave that man only had our name and phone number on it. That man agreed to let us rent his house without even knowing where we worked or even *if* we worked. Terrell, that man agreed to let us rent his house and he didn't even know our *name!*"

From that point on, there was no doubt in my mind about what was telling me to keep trying for the house. I knew that it was God. When I told Terrell, he totally agreed.

The house had a big backyard. Real big. All the way in the back of the yard was a basketball goal. We bought a volleyball set and put it up in the middle of the yard. Then we bought Terra a middle-sized swimming pool and put it near the back door, but there was still a lot of space, so guess what else we bought? A swing set! When Michael and Terrell got finished putting it together, I wanted to play on it so bad and probably would've if I wasn't so big that I might've tore it down. I could hardly sleep that night for looking out the window at it. . . .

That Fourth of July, I had a family reunion cookout in the backyard. We had a ball. The very next month, I had Terra's birthday party back there. Everything was almost perfect. Almost . . .

Chapter 35

Terrell went to the store one evening and ran into one of his old friends. When he left, he was wearing the Christmas present I'd bought for him, a leather coat. He didn't come home until the next day, and without the coat.

"What happened to your coat?" I asked him.

"I let some guy try it on, and he ran off with it."

It wasn't very hard for me to figure out what had happened, as much as I didn't want to believe it.

A few days later, I woke in time to find him quietly unplugging the VCR in our room.

"Where you going with that, Terrell?"

"I owe somebody some money and I don't have it."

"Well, you are just going to have to pay them back some other way, because that VCR ain't leaving this house."

"I'll buy another one when I get paid, Ivy. I just want to pay this man his money."

"No, you're not. You're going to have to pay this man when you get paid, because like I said, that VCR ain't leaving this house."

"Why don't you gone back to sleep, Ivy? I said I'll git another one."

"Why don't *you* go to sleep, because *I* said you ain't taking it!"

He tried to make believe he was going to bed until I went back to sleep, but then he tried to ease out again. I got up, put on some clothes, and went behind him. He looked at me like I was crazy. What I was getting ready to do was indeed crazy, although I didn't care at the moment.

"Where you think you going, woman?" That's what he called me whenever we argued—"woman."

"I'm going with you."

"For what, Ivy?"

"To pay this man his money and tell him not to give you nothing else on credit. That's for what."

In the front yard, I walked right by the van.

"We ain't riding?"

"Naw, we ain't riding!"

"I don't feel like walking all the way there."

I started to wonder how far was "all the way there" and felt that I really didn't feel like walking either. Before I knew it, I spun around and started yelling.

"You was getting ready to walk a few minutes ago carrying a VCR and now you can't walk carrying nothing? Get your dumb ass in the van, Terrell!"

When we got to the drug-infested neighborhood where Terrell told me to drive, I told him to go get this "man" he owed money to. Although I never got out of the van, I was still face-to-face with this man.

"I came to pay you the money that Terrell owes you, but let me tell you something," I said. "This is my *husband* and what's his is mine and when he tell you he got something at home, he's not talking about just *his* home, but *our* home. Ours *and* our children's."

The man gave me a look as if to say, "Who in the hell do you think you are? Are you crazy?" However, he didn't say a word until I was finished.

"I understand where you coming from, miss, but I gotta git mine, too."

I didn't back down.

"And I understand where *you* coming from, too, but all I'm telling you is that you don't need to give Terrell nothing else on credit, because when he runs out of money, that's *all* he got. He ain't got *nothing* else of his own at home, because if he did, he probably would've brought it with him when he came the first time."

The man said he understood. I think he was just ready to get me out of his face. When I was getting ready to pull off, Terrell started to get out of the van.

"Where you think *you* going?" I hissed at him.

"I'm just gonna hang around here for a little while to try to make your money back, Ivy," he said, never looking back.

I believed him. Because I had never done drugs myself, I was totally new to the game. It wasn't until much later that I learned that "ghetto dealers" didn't even extend credit. Terrell had probably tipped the man off to what I was going to say, the man had then gone along with the game to get more money out of Terrell, and whenever Terrell said he owed somebody some money for drugs he had already used, he was really getting money to buy more. . . .

Chapter 36

While I was pregnant with Terra, Bishop Edison died. It was the longest funeral and had the most people of any funeral I had ever been to in my life. There were numerous speakers including the mayor of the city, who said that there would be a Bishop Edison Day in honor of his memory. Bishop Edison was a very highly respected man who had accomplished a lot not only in the church, but also in the community.

After Bishop Edison died, the church really suffered. It needed a new pastor bad. When it finally got one, he was a much younger man. Everybody liked the new pastor, Pastor Jones, because he was so down to earth and cheerful all the time. He didn't pay too much attention to the stupid stuff and was just determined to be a good pastor. A lot of people joined the church and a lot of people who had previously left returned, including us.

I started working in the church again and, boy, did we have a lot of fun. I directed the youth choir and those kids could really sing. Pastor Jones also wanted a mass choir and I directed that too. The church choir never sounded as good before or since then. I'm not saying that because I was the director, but because it's true. Clarita even joined with us for a while and led the praise and worship part of the service. The pastor later asked Terrell to start working in the tape ministry, and he loved it. Later, Liz, along with another member of the church, started to direct the mass choir in my place, because Pastor Jones felt it was too much on me. Although this was true, I never complained because I loved it so much.

Mom said she enjoyed seeing her three daughters in the church working like that. She didn't mean that Clarita, Liz, and I were "all that" and couldn't be replaced; it's just that she knew that the Bible tells us that there are a lot of different parts to the body and each part depends on the others. I know, without a shadow of a doubt, that my family was blessed with musical abilities, and I thank God for us being able to share it with others, especially when it came to uplifting church services. Unfortunately, either everybody in the church did not understand this or else they just refused to accept it.

Clarita was first. She got a call from Pastor Jones telling her not to wear pants while she did praise and worship anymore. These were not pants that showed the shape of her crotch, now. Clarita was brought up in church and knew very well which kinds of pants were acceptable to wear to church and which were not. These were dressy pantsuits that Clarita had worn to work the night before so that she could come straight to church from work. Clarita said she was shocked, especially when Pastor

Jones said that it didn't bother *him,* but that there were several other church members whom it did bother. Clarita stopped wearing the pants, but it wasn't long before she just stopped coming altogether. She said she just couldn't stand being in bondage like that, and furthermore, like me, she wondered why it made such a difference what people wore if their heart was right.

Liz and I were next. We had a church business meeting and it seemed that a lot of petty stuff was going on in the choirs: we were showing favoritism and having disagreements about the musician and what the choir should and shouldn't be wearing when they sang. This. That. That. This. Hubba, hubba, hubba. Pastor Jones sat both of the choirs down during the meeting. I was hurt, but not because the choir that I directed was sat down like a lot of people thought. I was hurt because a lot of the young people loved singing in the choir so much, and truth be told, by that time the youth choir was all the young people had to take part in at church. Sure enough, when the youth choir was sat down, a lot of the young people lost interest and stopped coming to church. It really hurt Michael and Michelle, too.

"Dag, Ma, I don't even want to go to church anymore now," Michelle said to me after the business meeting.

"I know, man; it's gone be boring," said Michael.

Another time, the Sunday school was sponsoring an outing for the children of the church to the state fair. The superintendent of the Sunday school, who was Bishop Edison's widow, asked me for an idea for a fund-raiser and I said we should do a pageant.

Almost all of the children in the church were interested, because they knew that whenever I did anything with them, I went out of the way to make it different and interesting. We practiced hard. I fashioned it after the pageants that come on television with the casual wear, formal wear, and everything. They even did a little dance routine together, like the contestants on the television pageants, to a children's praise and worship song. Everyone was amazed at the way they remembered all the steps. I was so proud of them. I decided that the winners would be the boy and girl who raised the most money. I went to the trophy shop and bought mini-trophies, and Liz helped me (as she always did whenever I did anything for the children at church) by making certificates for all the children so that none of them would feel left out, but of course, the two winners' trophies were bigger and their certificates were different.

When the day of the pageant finally arrived, I don't know who was more excited, the children or myself. During Sunday school, the superintendent asked me if I had anything to say about it.

"Yes! First of all I'd like to thank you for giving me the opportunity to work with your children. They've worked so hard on this pageant and we are very excited and anxious to put it on, and if ya'll don't stay after church service to see it, you will really miss a treat!" Then a member of "the family" raised her hand. *Here we go,* I thought.

"Yes, I'd like to know if the bus is already paid for and if we have to pay our own way to get into the fair, what is this money being used for?" I immediately sensed danger but wasn't the least bit surprised.

"I'm not exactly sure, but I know it will be used in some way toward the trip. I just—"

"This is not the time to discuss that," the superintendent cut in. She didn't let them get to her as easily as I did.

No! Answer them! Please answer them! I was saying in my mind, because I knew what they were capable of. The superintendent did too, but she stood firm, determined not to be intimidated.

During halftime (that's what I called the little break between Sunday school and morning service), I saw some members of "the family" going into Pastor Jones's office. Although I wasn't sure of what was going to happen, I *was* sure that I was not going to like it. During morning service, right before Pastor Jones started preaching, he made comments and announcements about other things that were going on, like he did every Sunday. Then, sure enough, he started in on the pageant.

"Now as far as the pageant, we're still going to have it, but I don't want any money involved. Sister Ivy, all the money you've collected, just give it back to who you collected it from, and ain't nobody mad but the devil, amen." The last part of that statement couldn't have been further from the truth.

Of course "the family" answered the loudest.

"Amen!"

My head started to hurt. The emotions started to form a line, but when they saw Anger coming, they knew it was no use and all just parted, like the Red Sea did for Moses, to let Anger to the front.

"This don't make sense. I'm not having nothing. After church I'm going home," I said just loud enough for those around me to hear. I started giving the money back right then instead of waiting until after church. Some of the parents agreed with me and wouldn't even take the money back.

"I don't blame you, Ivy. I don't blame you," said Liz, who was sitting right behind me.

It was Communion Sunday and when they started to serve Communion, I went into the bathroom. Communion was something I took very seriously, even as a child, and I really don't think that a lot of people actually know how sacred taking Communion really is. In the scripture that was always read before we took it, it says that if people take it without being worthy to do so, they can get sick and even die. Then it tells us to examine ourselves so that we won't fall into this category. Then it says something that I know is not a joke, but I always thought was kind of funny: "If any man hungers, let him eat at home." Anyway, I went into the bathroom because I knew that I definitely was not worthy of taking Communion on this particular Sunday. I just couldn't understand how people so mean and devious could call themselves true Christians.

A few minutes later, Liz came into the bathroom with me. Of course, she was taught the same way I was about Communion, so I don't know if she came in there because she didn't want to take it either, or just to talk to me. Either way, it seemed as if she had changed her mind about what I should do about the pageant.

"Ivy, you know what?"

"What?"

"If I were you, I would still have it, because if you don't, you'll be doing exactly what they want you to do. Think about it; *you're* the one that's gonna look bad if you don't have it, because it'll hurt the children and they really want to do it and after all that's who it's really about, the children, right?" I didn't answer right away. I looked at the dresses that the girls had brought for their "formal wear" and had hung up in the bathroom. They were so pretty, particularly this white one that was full of ruffles and lace. It stood out all the way around the bottom like a ballroom gown. It was covered in a dry cleaner's bag.

"Think about it good, Ivy," Liz said, and then she was gone.

After church, the pageant was spectacular. They never had anything like it before or since then. I'm not saying this because I'm the one who directed it, but because it's true.

Soon a lot of the members stopped coming to church because it seemed that the people didn't really have love for each other like they should. Everybody was hurting everybody's feelings and nobody seemed to care. Pastor Jones preached sermon after sermon on "love," and the more he preached, the worse things got. The business meetings turned into meetings where people told each other off, and the hatred and tension were so thick it was almost unbelievable. Once during a business meeting, Pastor Jones asked if anybody else had anything to say before he closed and Michelle stood up. *My* Michelle.

"I'd just like to say that I think it's sad that we can't love each other like we should and stop all this petty fussing and fighting over stupid stuff. . . ." She paused because she started crying. When she started talking again, she was yelling at the top of her lungs.

"It don't make no sense the way we acting and we need to stop!"

Half of the people were looking at Michelle and the other half at me. I had mixed emotions about making her be quiet, because in a way I did feel like Michelle was out of order, but I decided to let her continue for two reasons. The first is that Michelle and Michael, like their mother, grandmother, great-grandmother, and so on, loved church. I never had to "make" them go, like a lot of other parents did their children. As a matter of fact, I can remember times when my children made *me* go. I knew that Michelle was deeply hurt by what was happening and she needed to get it out. The second reason is that there's a verse in the Bible that says, "A child shall lead them. . . ." I thought that if the church members could see what kind of an effect they were having on the youth of the church, they would somehow be shamed into stopping the drama. As I had so many other times, though, I had thought wrong.

Chapter 37

From the first time Terrell went "back on the streets," my marriage had me on a serious emotional roller coaster. I still loved Terrell with all my heart, and I kept thinking that if only I could keep him off the street and away from the drugs, he would be the husband he was in the beginning. I was determined to keep trying, although deep inside I knew I was fighting a losing battle.

Eventually, he started showing signs of being unfaithful. I couldn't take it anymore and told him he had to leave the house. I missed him so much, but I knew that the peace that I would have without him would be so much more important. He missed us too, because every time I turned around he was coming over to visit.

Once when he was leaving, he went outside in the backyard to say good-bye to Terra, who was playing on the swing set. I stood in front of the dining room window and watched him as he picked her up and put her on the top of the sliding board so that they could be on the same eye level. I continued to watch as he talked to her, and although I knew that she couldn't understand everything that he was saying, she never took her eyes off of him. Then they hugged. My eyes clouded with tears. At that point, my feelings changed. Until then, I had wanted Terrell to be home because I loved him so much, but after I watched them in the backyard, I wanted him home for the baby. *Our* baby.

When he came back home, things were better, but only for a while. It wasn't long before he was back to staying out all night either doing drugs, running women, or both. The only thing good about Terrell was that he always worked. From listening to Terrell talk about his "associates," I learned that there are drug users who just steal for their drugs, and then there are those who are fortunate enough to have someone else support their habit, and last there are those who actually work every day. I think that the last group is the hardest kind to figure out, because it makes you wonder how they can take their hard-earned money and throw it down the drain like that or how their employers don't test them and catch them or something.

Terrell worked hard every day and sometimes he would take his whole check to get high with. Then, because he knew he was wrong for what he'd done, he would take his next check and catch everything up. I kept on trying to explain to him that the money that he was using to play catch-up with was the same money that we could be using to get ahead. He said that he understood, but the next week, he'd just go through the routine all over again.

Once when we were having one of our heart-to-heart talks and he was explaining to me how hard it was to stop, I started to think about how many other people I knew who had lost their jobs, families, friends, and even their children behind it. I started to wonder if it could possibly be that good. I said something that totally shocked Terrell and I can imagine just how much, because I even shocked myself when I said it.

"Bring some home."

"What?"

"You heard me. Bring me some and let me try it."

"Is you done gone crazy, woman?"

"No, I just think that it's got to be some awfully good stuff the way people be losing their jobs, families, friends, homes, cars, and their very minds over it, so I want to try it. Just one time."

"Naw, I can't do it, Ivy. Your family would hate me forever if I did that."

"My family?"

"Yeah, because it wouldn't be just once. You'd get hooked, just as sure as hell, and it'll be all my fault for bringing it to you in the first place."

I figured as well as Terrell knew me, and as well as he knew cocaine, he also probably knew what he was talking about, so I never asked again. Then I started to feel real bad because real deep inside I knew that if I tried hard enough, eventually I could've convinced Terrell to bring me some cocaine. Then when I thought about how things would've turned out if I really had gotten hooked, it hurt. I mean it really hurt so much that I actually felt a pain in my heart when I thought about it hard enough.

The twins reacted to him totally differently. Of course, Michelle was very opinionated and had no problem letting him know how she felt about him and the things he was doing. Michael, on the other hand, was very quiet. I mean, he never said anything. Nothing. I used to worry about this, because of the cliché "It's the quiet ones that you have to watch, because you never know what they're thinking about doing until they've done it, and by then it's too late."

Once when I was asleep, I woke up to the sound of fussing. At the end of the hall, I could only see Michelle's back. Every once in a while, Terrell would peek out from behind Michelle and tell me to make her get out of his way. He had taken the VCR out of our bedroom and was holding it in his arm like a child holding a school notebook. Evidently he was going to take it out and sell it.

"I don't care *what* Momma say, *I* say you ain't taking it *nowhere*, so put it *back!*" My eyebrows rose when I heard her say that she didn't care what I said, but my curiosity about how her and Terrell's battle would turn out got the best of me and I was quiet.

"You better move out my way, Michelle. I'm not playing."

Michelle was like a tree planted by the water.

"I'm not playing either, so you might as well put it back. Don't make no sense, you taking electrical appliances out the house like you some kind of electrical appliance salesman or something trying to support your drug habit. You won't do it *this* night, so you might as well put it back. Put it back, plug it back up, and *re*-program it."

It was so pitiful, but, on the other hand, it was kind of funny, because Michelle was standing there with one hand on her hip and the other hand pointing into the room that they were standing in front of while she spat out the demands like she was Terra's momma.

"Ivy!" Terrell kept calling me, but I wouldn't answer. Eventually, Terrell went back into the room, slammed the VCR on the bed, and packed a bag to stay out all night. Michelle went back into her room and went back to bed, and I went on back to sleep. It was just like nothing had ever happened, because by this time, things like this happened so often that it was a regular routine.

Although Michael was quiet during all these blowouts we were having, he still stood close by in case things got physical. Once when Mom was over at our house, things got heated because Terrell took the van after he had been drinking. When he got back, I tried to get him to give me the keys but he wouldn't. When I threatened to call the police, he threw the keys out into the yard and we couldn't find them, because it was dark. Michelle started in on him again, as Michael just silently sat on the couch.

"Don't make no sense, Terrell. You always doing something you ain't got no business doing!"

Things got so heated that Terrell acted like he was going to hit Michelle. The reason I mentioned that Mom was over was that she walked with a cane. Michael never said anything. He just got up, got Mom's cane, and went and sat back down.

"Oh, and what you think you supposed to do with that?" Terrell asked Michael.

"I ain't say nothing to you," was all Michael said, in a quiet, even tone while swinging the cane. Terrell talked a little more trash and then he was gone. He might have been high, but he wasn't crazy.

Once when we were talking, Terrell said that I

was wrong for including my children in everything and that they were spoiled and disrespectful.

"Well, Terrell, it's mighty funny that you never felt this way before you started 'showing' yourself. And furthermore, if my children were really disrespectful like you say, they would've hurt you a long time ago, because very rarely do you hear of children this big (by then they were both over six feet tall) who were raised in the projects letting the men in their mother's life abuse them like you do me."

"Abuse you? Ivy, how can you say that I abuse you when I never laid a hand on you or even so much as called you out of your name?" It was hard to believe, considering all of the arguments that we'd had, but up to this point, he really never had done either of those two things. Anyway, I loved it when he asked me questions like this, because it gave us the opportunity to have another one of our heart-to-heart conversations. It was during these conversations that he admitted that what I said made a lot of sense. This was, of course, until he got drunk or high again.

"Terrell, do you remember that time you got beat up?"

"You trying to be funny, woman. You know good and well I remember that beating."

"Come here. . . ."

It had been a typical workday for Terrell and when he got home, he was hot and tired. After he came in, showered, and put on clean clothes, he went out the door.

"I be right back. I'm going to the store and put my numbers in." This was what he did every day. Sometimes he did

come right back. Sometimes he came back a few hours later. Sometimes he came back in the middle of the night. Sometimes he didn't make it back until the next morning.

This particular night was probably going to be a "next morning" event, only during the middle of the night I received a phone call from his mom.

"Ivy." His mom's voice sounded kind of shaken. Oh, Lord, *I thought,* what has that crazy man gotten into now?

"Yes?"

"Terrell want to know if you can come get him."

"Ask him how did he get there."

"He got beat up, Ivy."

"What?"

"Some guys got him and beat him up real bad."

Because it was the first time that this had happened while we were together, I didn't realize how serious it really was. I knew that Terrell had gotten into a few spats here and there with the neighbors, but by the very next night, he'd be right out there drinking and laughing with them again. Besides, I thought, maybe this would teach him a lesson about hanging out in the street instead of being at home with his family, where he belonged. At this point, I was hoping anything would be some kind of help.

"Naw, I gotta go to work in a couple of hours. I'm tired of having to jump up behind Terrell acting simple all the time."

"Okay, bye."

"Bye."

When I came home from work the next day, Terrell was there sitting on the couch. When I saw him, I almost fainted. He looked like a monster. His head was swollen real big on one side and gashed open on top. His lips were swollen and busted too. One eye was completely shut and the other one was blackened. He didn't say anything; he just looked at me.

My knees were shaking so bad, I sat in the chair that was nearest to me as I stared back at him in disbelief. The Line of Emotions formed. Very slowly this time. Slower than it ever had before, and I had plenty of time to entertain each one of them. I couldn't take it anymore, and although what I said to him couldn't have been said at a worse time, I felt that if I didn't say it right then, I was going to bust.

"Look at you, Terrell. This don't make no sense. If you can't get yourself together and stop taking me and the children through these kinds of changes, you really need to leave for good."

"After I got beat up like this, Ivy, is that all you can think of to say to me?"

"You heard me, Terrell. I can't take this mess no more," I said as I walked out of the room trying real hard not to look back at him. I tried hard to go to sleep, because I was so tired from working all night, but every time I closed my eyes, I could see Terrell on the ground with those guys beating him in the face, and my eyes would come back open.

Again I thought about the time I looked for the red blouse in my room in Cleveland about thirty-five years before, then wondered how I'd made it through all that mess. . . .

Then we were standing in our bedroom in front of the dresser mirror.

"You remember how you looked after they beat you, Terrell?"

"Yeah."

"Can you see any scars from the beating now?"

He paused before he answered.

"Naw."

"I know you can't Terrell, because God designed

our bodies so that they're self-healing. Lots of times if we get any cuts and bruises, as long as they're not too serious, in time they completely go away."

"Okay . . ."

"But what you don't understand is that there's more than one kind of abuse. Terrell, some of the things you've put me through since you started running the street and doing drugs again, I'll never forget. And it hurts. It really hurts. And you act like you don't care, so that makes what you're doing to me a form of abuse. Abuse doesn't always have to be physical. It can be mental or emotional too, and these kinds are even worse, because they are the ones that you can't bounce back from as quickly. They take much longer to heal. Sometimes they *never* do."

"Yeah, I see where you coming from," was all Terrell could say.

This is why now (as well as then) the cliché that takes first place with me as far as being the biggest lie ever told to man is "Sticks and stones may break my bones, but words will never hurt me." I feel that whoever made up this saying must have never experienced mental or emotional abuse, and anyone who has ever *really* thought about it and also *really* knows me knows that I'm not just saying this because I've been mentally and emotionally hurt, but because it's true.

Although I should have easily been able to decide what to do about my marriage, I still couldn't. We decided to go to Pastor Jones for counseling. No one was in the pastor's office except Terrell, the pastor, his wife, and me. The following week, almost every word that was spoken in the session was repeated to me by another lady in the church. It was also told to the lady that I was stupid for staying with Terrell, because if it were them, they wouldn't do it. Church people . . .

When I talked to my closest friends about Terrell, who at that time were Medina, Johnice, Mildred, and Gloria, they never said anything. They knew that the ultimate decision about what to do about my marriage was my own, so they just quietly listened while I vented. Sometimes I would get frustrated with them, because they wouldn't offer their opinions, but now when I think about it, they were just being the kind of friends that I really needed at the time.

Chapter 38

Whenever I finished talking to Gloria, she would turn the conversation around so that we would be talking about how I could make life better for myself.

Gloria and Patrice dropped out of school soon after I did, but after they were married, they both went back to college and got their bachelor's degrees. Gloria used to do all she could to convince me to do the same. She promised me that once I did, I would see life a whole lot differently. I told her that it was easy for her and Patrice, because besides the fact that they both had jobs with nice incomes, she was married to a retired serviceman and Patrice's husband, Rueben, was on the management team of a very well-known manufacturing company. Both Rueben and Doug (Gloria's husband) were good providers for their families. I, on the other hand, had to work whenever and wherever I could and was married to a crackhead who sometimes acted like he didn't care whether our baby and I lived or died. . . .

Once when I applied for a job, the interviewer

requested that I provide my college transcripts. When I sent away to Virginia State for them, they wouldn't send them to me because they insisted that I still owed the school money.

"How can they say they don't send transcripts until all of my fees are paid when they sent them to me before to apply for another job back in ninety-one? I haven't been back there to take any classes since then!" I was on the phone with Gloria, who I referred to as my business adviser, because she was so cool when it came to situations like that.

"Girl, please. You know you can't handle nothing like that on the phone. You have to go up there. I'll take a day off next week and go with you. If we leave as soon as we put the kids on the bus, we should be back before they get back home. What day did you want to go?"

When we first got to Virginia State, we couldn't resist touring the campus and reminiscing about when we were students there. Right when we started to go into the office to get my transcripts, we heard drums. Sure enough, it was the band marching toward the football field for practice. It brought back so many good memories.

In the financial office, there was a young girl behind the counter who told me the same story about the transcripts.

"I'm sorry, ma'am, but our records show that you still have outstanding fees, so you won't be able to get the transcripts until they are paid." I argued with the girl while Gloria stayed in the background saying nothing. When I looked to Gloria for help, she was going out the door behind a much older lady who had come from behind the counter to go to the restroom.

By the time I thanked the young girl and followed Gloria and the older lady into the restroom, Gloria was almost finished telling the older lady the whole story of how I had stopped going to Virginia State around twenty years ago, how I had applied for a job about ten years ago and asked for the transcripts and got them, and how we had both taken the day off from our jobs for the two-hour drive to come there and get it straight. . . .

After she finished listening to Gloria, the older lady told us to go to the store and get the two-dollar money order transcript fee, and when we came back, to give it to *her.* Gloria had me cracking up talking about the young girl and the old lady when we got back in the van to go to the store.

"Girl, please. You know you can't deal with them young girls. They so happy financial aid gave them a job that makes them feel like they have some kind of authority. They probably be telling people no just because they can. You have to deal with the head people in those kinds of offices. The ones that been there for about a hundred years that *know* how to get around the rules. Girl, please."

The store was the very same store that we'd walked to at night so many years ago to get snacks to eat in Patrice's room. . . .

About five minutes after we came back from the store and gave the lady the two-dollar money order, we were on our way back home with my transcripts. When we got to the interstate exit where we were supposed to get off and go to my house, Gloria glanced at her watch and kept on going.

"Where we going now?" I asked.

"You'll see," Gloria replied, never looking my way.

When we pulled onto the campus of the local community college, I immediately knew what she was trying to do.

"Gloria, I really can't do this right now. I—"

"Girl, will you please shut up and come on?" She was out of the van and on her way to the office building, with me following behind her and complaining like I was her child or something. I guess it did look funny, because I was at least a foot and a half taller than she was.

She had me standing in the line to register for classes while she ran to the admissions and financial aid office and brought me all kinds of papers.

"Fill this out. . . . Now fill this out. Hurry up."

"Gloria, I can't. . . ."

"Will you please stop talking about what you can't do and fill the papers out so you'll be finished before the lady gets to you?"

I snatched the papers from her and filled them out, while the people around us laughed. When we left, I only had one class, which was the orientation class, but it was official—I was back in college.

Chapter 39

Terra was invited to the birthday party of a child of one of Liz's coworkers who was turning two years old. It was in March, and that August, Terra would be turning three. The party went well and the parents had just as much fun with each other as the children did. I couldn't take my eyes off Terra, because I didn't want her to hurt herself by playing too roughly or soil her clothes by eating too messily. Slowly it dawned on me that something wasn't right, though, because none of the other children needed their mothers to continuously wipe their mouths although all of them were younger than Terra. When the children wanted more to eat or drink, I noticed that they asked for it more plainly than Terra. When we all went outside for an Easter egg hunt, I noticed that I was the only parent who had to hold her child by the hand and help her find eggs. All of these children were younger than Terra and these things started to puzzle me, especially the difference in their speech development. I started to get scared. Something was definitely not right. . . .

The next time I took Terra to her pediatrician for her routine checkup and was asked if I had any concerns, I told her that Terra wasn't talking.

"She's not talking?" the doctor asked, with a frown on her face.

"Well, she can talk, but I don't think she's talking as well as she should be for her age," I answered, with raised shoulders.

The doctor started to ask Terra questions like what colors were in her clothes. I couldn't figure out if she was trying to find out if Terra actually knew the colors, or if she was just listening to how Terra pronounced the names of the colors. When she finished asking Terra the questions, she agreed with me and referred Terra to a specialist for further testing. I tried to listen to her carefully as she described what testing procedures would be used, but her voice kept fading in and out as my mind kept drifting. *Not* my *baby. She can't be talking about* my *baby,* I couldn't stop thinking.

The first series of tests weren't all that bad, although Terra got tired of them and stopped participating. First she was asked to walk up a short flight of steps. Instead of alternating her feet on each step, she kept leading off to the next step with the same foot, like a toddler who was first learning to climb steps. Then they asked her to pour water from one container to another but she couldn't. Next they asked her to walk on her tiptoes and she couldn't. Then they asked her to stand on one foot and she couldn't.

As the tests continued, I watched and I tried hard to fight back the tears. I was angry for not noticing these things earlier. The doctor assured me that it wasn't my fault, because it had been so long since

I'd previously had children that I'd probably forgotten about the proper stages of childhood development. Then she referred Terra for further testing. As she described the next series of tests to me, I couldn't fight the tears any longer.

When I got home, I couldn't stop shaking. I finally calmed my nerves enough to call my mother. She listened as I told her what the doctor told me.

". . . And if it's God's will that she's this way, I know that I have to accept it, but . . ." I broke down crying again. I was so shaken, I couldn't remember what my mother had said to encourage me.

When Terrell came home from work that day, I told him what had happened. He didn't say anything, just stared at me as I finished talking and began to cry again. He said that Terra was our baby and assured me that we would pull through it together.

"I believe we can too, Terrell, but only if you stop the drinking, drugs, and other women, because all this is too much for me to handle."

"I will. I promise."

Chapter 40

I asked Gloria to go with me to Terra's next appointment because I was more than sure that I wouldn't be able to stay with her as they did all kinds of scans, blood drawings, and God knows what other kinds of pokings and probings. By this time, Gloria had three children of her own and was the type of mother who was totally calm about everything her children did as long as they weren't killing themselves or each other.

"Ivy, I understand what the people are saying about Terra, but there're still a lot of things that Terra probably *could* do if you'd just stop being so overprotective. Just put the girl outside and let her play with other kids. You'd be surprised what she'll learn," Gloria told me one day. Then she had me laughing about how her youngest son, DJ, knew how to ride a bicycle without training wheels when he was still in Pampers.

When we first got to the hospital where Terra's appointment was, I had to fill out at least twenty different forms, and then the nurse took Terra's weight, height, blood pressure, and stuff like that. Then we were put in a room and waited for what seemed like hours. Finally, a young yet plain-looking lady came in. I thought she was coming to bring me more papers or something until she reached out to shake my hand and introduced herself as Terra's genetic specialist. Immediately I began to form opinions about the lady. *You can't be; you're much too young to be* any *kind of specialist, and where is your doctor's coat and what is a genetic specialist anyway?* It was almost as if she read my mind, because she started answering the questions that were running through it.

"I don't wear a lab coat because most children automatically relate them to doctors and become afraid. What we're going to do first is go over the questions that you answered on this form and then I'll give you a chance to address any other concerns you may have before we do any more testing." Then she smiled and looked down. "And is this Terra?"

She was right about the lab coat, because Terra was terrified of doctors, but she warmed up to the specialist instantly and answered all of her questions without any problems. The specialist then asked me more questions, then took out a tape measure and began to measure Terra's head, hands, fingers, feet, and even the space between her eyes. She then asked me more questions, then asked Terra more questions, then asked me more questions. I thought it would never end. She left the room and soon came back with some papers in her hand. She said that Terra showed evidence of having something called Prader-Willi syndrome. I was concentrating so hard on what she was saying that I wasn't looking in her face but instead in her very mouth. I started asking questions that now when I think about it didn't sound too intelligent, but at the time I didn't care. I wanted a full understanding and I just started blurting out every question that came to mind.

"Is that anything like Down's syndrome?"

"No. It's totally different. With Down's syndrome, there's an extra chromosome in the genetic makeup. With Prader-Willi, the count is correct, but one of the sets is defective. It's called Prader-Willi because those are the names of the two doctors who are doing the research on it. The chromosome deficiency causes a universal delay."

"Universal delay?"

"Yes, this means that she will be behind in every area of her development."

"In every area?"

It seemed that I should have gotten on her nerves by repeating everything she said like that, but I didn't. I guess she had experienced this so many times before with other parents.

"Yes, this means her mental as well as her physical development. Now, when I say physical I mean her motor skills, not her actual body parts. Her speech . . . These children are obese because their minds tell them that they're hungry when they're not. . . . Lifelong disability . . ."

Her voice started to fade in and out as I thought about Terra not being able to stand on one foot or walk on her tiptoes, and still saying "eat-eat" at the birthday party, and the time she left home. . . .

* * *

It was a typical day. Terrell was still at work, the twins were just coming home from school, I was in the living room watching TV, and Terra was in her room playing. I had worked the night before and was really tired. After the twins grabbed a snack they were out the door again.

"Ma, we gone." *Michael was taking Michelle to work.*

"Okay. Be careful, now."

"Okay."

I watched them go out the door. They had grown up so fast. I could still clearly remember the nurse bringing them in to me the very first time with the blue and pink caps on, and now they were driving, almost finished high school, and working.

I was so glad to see that the lessons I had taught them in finances had paid off. Michelle was ever so careful when she got her paychecks, always looking for a bargain. Michael wasn't as eager to bargain shop because he favored the name-brand stuff, so he learned how to save in other ways. Once when we were shopping I noticed that he went out of his way to pay for everything he bought with the exact change.

"Why you gotta take so long looking for change when you can give the lady bills?" *I asked him.*

"I know," *Michelle agreed with me.* "He always holding the line up digging for pennies."

"Because I'm trying to save my little money," *he answered, with a laugh.*

"Save? You a little too late for that, ain't you? You tried to buy the highest things the people had in the store."

"But still, though—think about it. If I give the people my change, the longer I can keep my ones. The longer I keep my ones, the longer I can keep my fives. The longer I keep my fives, the longer I can keep my tens. . . ." *Michelle and I both laughed at him, saying that in the end it still came out to spending the same amount. Soon we started doing the same thing, though, and found that it was indeed true. . . .*

I felt someone put both hands on both of my knees. When I opened my eyes, it was Michael, with his face no more than six inches from mine. I would've thought no more than a few minutes had passed, but it had to be at least an hour, because Michelle's job was at least a half hour away. I'll never forget the sound of Michael's voice or what he said. Never.

"Ma, where's Terra?"

"I don't . . ."

He was out the door before I finished. I was right behind him. He ran in one direction and I in the other, yelling Terra's name as loud as we could. My face was drenched with a combination of sweat and tears as I stopped yelling her name and started yelling a prayer.

"Oh my god! Please protect my baby! God, please don't let anyone harm her! God, please, please bring her back home to me safe! Oh, God, in the name of Jesus, please bring her home!!!"

I was out of breath as I turned to walk back home. I started to pray again. This time much more softly. "God, I can't take any more. You promised that you would put no more on me than I could bear and I can't take any more. I can't . . ."

Way down the street, I could see Michael coming toward me, still running. When he was sure that I could see him, he pointed behind me. When I turned around again, there was Terra coming around the corner of the 7-Eleven with a man. I ran back to the corner.

"Thank you so much," I barely managed to say, because I was almost completely out of breath.

"Oh, you're welcome," the man said, smiling. "I was asking her her name and where she lived, but I couldn't understand what she was saying. . . ."

* * *

I don't know if she meant to, but Gloria bumped me. I struggled to bring my mind back to what the genetic specialist was saying.

". . . So here's some information about it that should answer more questions you may have, along with my card so that you can talk to me personally if you feel that you need to. Also, you can check other resources like books and the Internet. Please don't forget that there are thousands of children like her, so you probably won't have any trouble finding different support groups in your area. Now, you'll need to take this paperwork down to the lab to have her other test done and you'll be all finished, but please stop by the front desk so that the receptionist can schedule Terra's next appointment." She was smiling as she spoke. Then she said, "Bye, Terra."

"Bye," Terra replied.

"See, that wasn't so bad, right, Terra? Now if you be a big girl in the other doctor's office, we'll go to the cafeteria to get you a special treat, okay?" Gloria then said to Terra.

I was thankful she was there, because I don't know how I would've made it without her. Everyone was smiling except me. Once again, I was deep in thought about what had happened in that room at 254 N. Vine Aveue in Cleveland, Ohio, over thirty-five years ago and wondering if I would ever finish paying for it. . . .

Chapter 41

As soon as Terrell had me believing that he was going to change, he started showing off again. It seemed like each time he did something and I forgave him, he came back and did something even worse. What hurt the most was that before I even realized it, I was doing what I promised myself I would never do, which was put a man before my peace of mind and the peaceful home that I worked so hard to have for Michael and Michelle in the past.

At the place where I worked at that time, we could basically choose our own hours, and soon I found myself working almost around the clock to pay all of our bills. A family member who had previously gone through the same thing with her husband told me that I was "enabling" Terrell, because as long as I paid all the bills, he would continue to blow his money getting high. I didn't want to keep doing that, but I also didn't want to lose the house or have our utilities turned off. I didn't know what to do but didn't have to think about it too long because I was soon fired for sleeping on the job. After that, things really started going downhill fast. . . .

Once I left Terrell and went to stay with Liz for a while. Liz decorated her house with exotic and odd African pieces: animals, dolls, masks, candles in candleholders, musical instruments, clocks, mirrors, and the whole nine. I soon decided to go back home, though, because I had to try too hard to keep Terra under control so that she wouldn't break too many of Liz's things. On top of that, it just didn't seem fair to deprive Terra of all her play space she had at home just because Terrell didn't know how to act. As soon as Terrell got home the evening following our return and saw us there, I let him have it.

"I didn't come back home for you, Terrell, but for Terra."

"I don't care why you came back, Ivy; I'm just glad that you did." Then he told the lie that I'd heard him tell so many times before. "And don't worry, Ivy, it'll be different this time."

Another time Terrell got drunk and started showing off and finally "called me out my name." He started walking toward me with his fist balled like he was going to hit me, and Michelle came up behind him screaming that he had better not do it. Michael was standing against the wall silent, as usual, but ready to defend us if we needed to be. Sure enough, Terrell turned around and pushed Michelle, and quick as a flash, Michael grabbed him and slammed him on the dining room table. Needless to say, the dining room table was destroyed. Terrell struggled to get up, but Michael was too strong for him. Every time Terrell tried to so much as move, Michael would use one of the wrestling moves he'd learned to make him lie still. Michelle called the cops and Michael *never said a word*, just held him there until the cops came.

While the cop was there listening to our stories, Terrell got so mad that he ran and got the hammer and started to tear up everything in the house, starting with the giant screen TV that we had worked so hard for. I begged the cop to make him stop, but the cop said he couldn't because Terrell was tearing up his own stuff. I couldn't believe it. When the cop couldn't take any more, he finally made Terrell stop, get some things, and leave the house. After he left and all was quiet, no one said anything for about a solid hour. We all just looked at the house and cried. Even Michael, who I hadn't seen shed a tear since he was a little boy, threw himself across his bed crying and said that he couldn't take it anymore. Within a month, everything Terrell had destroyed, he replaced.

Another time, he started going with this particular lady who was bold enough to call the house whenever she wanted to talk to him, but Terrell would always get to the phone first and would either tell her he'd call her back or leave the house. We got in an argument once and he left and went over to this same lady's house, and then had the audacity to call me from her house to ask me to come and get him.

"Terrell, have you lost your mind?"

"What?"

"Where are you calling me from?"

Silence.

"Terrell!"

"Gwen's."

I asked him to put her on the phone and he didn't have any more sense than to do it.

"Hello?"

I couldn't believe her nerve. Or his nerve. Or my stupidity. The whole thing.

"Hi, Gwen. This is Ivy *Smith.*" I said the last name as hard as I could. "How are you?"

"I'm okay, I—"

"Listen, Gwen. I want to tell you that my gripe is not with you, because as long as we let Terrell do this to us, he's going to do it, but let me ask you something. Doesn't it break your heart each time he does it? I mean, I know that you *have* to care for him to let him keep coming there every time we have an argument, but do you love my husband *that* much?"

Gwen then said something that put me at a complete loss for words like I had never been before or have since. Her voice was low and even toned, but firm enough to make me believe that she meant what she said with every fiber of her being.

"Yes, I do."

Another time, Terrell kept coming in and out of the house for about two days straight. Each time he would go in our bedroom and take God knows what out. When he left, I would go back there and try to find what was missing. Finally, I got tired of it and the next time he came in, I started yelling at him at the top of my lungs. I'd never fussed at him so long and hard before. All of a sudden I started having very bad chest pains and my legs started getting weak. I fell to the floor. Michelle called the ambulance and Michael held me in his arms until it arrived.

"Hang in there, Ma. Please hang in there, Ma,"

Michael kept repeating. At the hospital, the doctors ran tests on my heart and told me that I didn't have a heart attack, but that my heart was overstressed, which could easily lead to an attack if I didn't slow down. Michelle called Liz and she came to the hospital right away. She stood by my bed rubbing my back.

"Ivy, please don't let this man drive you crazy."

"I won't," I got up enough strength to say. I couldn't stop crying, though, because, thinking back on the peaceful life I had with the twins before I met him, I was afraid that I already had. Liz never left my side the whole time. Never before or since have I felt that much love from my sister Liz. . . .

When I came home I had a long talk with Michelle, who wanted to know why and how long I was going to let Terrell take me through all the drama.

"I don't know Michelle, I don't know."

"What you mean, you don't know?"

Michelle was a headstrong person who believed in saying what was on her mind, and most of the time, I couldn't decide if this was a bad or good thing.

"I mean I don't know. Let me explain. . . ."

"Please."

I tried hard to ignore her sarcasm, because I knew that she had a legitimate gripe.

"You remember how Brother and Sister Wilson from church were just in the newspaper for celebrating their fiftieth wedding anniversary? Well, I know for a fact that those fifty years weren't easy. I know for a fact that they had to go through a whole lot of stuff in those fifty years. A *whole lot* of stuff. Now, do you remember Treva and Tobias, who just got married last month? Well, they've already separated. So to answer your question, Michelle, between those two extremes, every woman has her own limits as to how much she can take. *Every* woman. And I'm not sure why, but, for some reason, I haven't reached my limit yet and people may think I'm stupid, but nobody can say what they will or won't do until *they* go through it themselves. But, Michelle, one thing's for sure—when I finally do leave here, nobody's going to be able to say that I didn't give this marriage a fair chance. Nobody."

Michelle didn't say anything, but her facial expression let me know that she understood.

I've always learned that prayer does two things: it either changes a situation, or changes people so that they can deal with the situation. When it came to Terrell, a lot of times I felt that God was doing both. Especially when I thought of how I met Quanda.

It's really amazing how God puts someone in your path when you need that person most, but you don't even realize it until after you've met the person. I was working at a hotel one day at the lowest point of my "roller coaster" ride with Terrell. Quite naturally, I was thinking of whatever drama I was going through with him at that time, and then I started to cry and couldn't stop. While cleaning this particular room, the lady who the room belonged to came in. She had just finished jogging. Her name was Quanda. She was a very beautiful person, and soon after talking to her, I found that it wasn't only on the outside. Although my eyes were all puffy and red from crying, she never asked me what was wrong. Nevertheless, I was so full of what I was thinking that before I knew it, I was pouring it all out to her.

What am I doing telling this lady all my business like this when I don't know her from a can of paint? I kept thinking. Still, I somehow couldn't stop myself from talking as Quanda listened with all the patience in the world. I told her about how I felt that I had messed up my life beginning with not taking my college education seriously and ending with the current drama with Terrell.

When Quanda finally started to talk back to me, she never responded to anything I told her. Instead, she only talked about how I could (and she didn't stress *should,* but *could*) rebuild myself physically, mentally, and emotionally. After my conversation with Quanda, I felt like a totally new person. We exchanged numbers and planned to get together soon but never did. Still, I never will forget Quanda or the things she told me, because at that point, I was so broken spiritually and the more I thought about it, the more I was sure that God had sent her to me so that I could *physically* hear what He wanted me to know. . . .

Chapter 42

Michael and Michelle were graduating from high school. I couldn't sleep the night before for trying to remember something they did special each school year. I let my mind go all the way back to the very first day of First Step, the big yellow bus, and the He-Man and Cabbage Patch lunch boxes, and then to all the noise they made with the other kids on the school bus as they got off in front of the house for the very last time.

I even thought about the two events that I'd regretted missing the most while they were in school. One was Michelle's second-grade spelling bee championship. She won. Then all of the winners of all the second-grade classes in the school went against each other. Michelle won that too. Last, all the winners in the second grade in the city went against each other in a spelling bee. Michelle came home with a plaque. On it were her name, the school, the year, and a bee holding a banner that said "spelling." I was so proud of her I could've cried. About the same time, she had broken her arm and had a cast on it.

She also had just started wearing eyeglasses. Lydia said to win the spelling bee, Michelle had to spell *orthopedic*. That woman was so crazy.

The other event was Michael's wrestling tournament. I was never too crazy about wrestling. I thought of wrestling as a "white boy" sport, even though one of the guys I dated in high school was the state champion. I had gone to one of Michael's regular matches at the high school and he lost. Every time the boy threw Michael down, Michael would look up at me in embarrassment. I thought he did pretty well, but the boy was just too strong for him. I think it was one of those situations like when he played Little League football. Because of Michael's weight, he was put in the same category as team members who had participated on the team the previous year and it was only Michael's first year. I made up my mind not to go anymore, because I didn't want him to worry about me being there seeing him lose any matches. I felt like I had supported him enough during the football seasons anyway, especially during his senior year, when he was captain of the team. Anyway, a few weeks later at the end of the wrestling season, Michael went out of town to the district championship tournament. When he came home, he had a poster with the sideways tournament tree on it, a trophy, and a blue ribbon. He didn't say anything, just went straight to bed. On the poster, I found his name on the widest row of branches and kept seeing it on each column as the branches narrowed. When there were no more branches and only the trunk, his name was there. Then I picked up the trophy. On the gold plate, it read MICHAEL WILLIAMS, 2000 DISTRICT CHAMPION HEAVYWEIGHT DIVISION. He took first place in the district. The next morning, we laughed at him and said that he must have been awfully tired from being thrown around all day since he couldn't even talk about it when he got home, much as he always ran his mouth.

Although school was all over for the twins, it was just beginning for Terra, who was scheduled to start that September in a program called PEEP, which stood for Program for Educating Exceptional Preschoolers.

I thought a lot about the twins and wondered if it would ever get to the point where I wouldn't have to worry about them so much. I really wanted to call them more often, but I knew how unhappy Michelle was and I couldn't stand to hear her complain. She had started to use any excuse she could to come home, including her not getting along with her dad. Michael told me that they once got into a yelling match while their faces were only about an inch apart. This wasn't hard for me to believe, because I knew how headstrong Michelle was, but I also knew that James wasn't going to let Michelle take over his house.

"How he think he can tell me so much now when he wasn't there for me when I needed him the most?" she once asked me. As usual, Michelle had a legitimate gripe, and the sad part about it was that to that day I was *still* fighting James for my back child support! But as always, I tried to make her use her "smartness" to her advantage.

"Well, Michelle, if that's the way you feel, then the only thing for you to do is let him do everything he wants to do for you now. Let him help you through college until you have every degree that he has. Then you can show him that if you have children and their father disappears like he did, you can still take good care of the children by yourself. Don't fight him about the past, Michelle; fight him for your future." I was so tired of fussing with her, and there were even other people sticking their nose in it, telling me that if her heart wasn't in it, then I shouldn't make her stay there. I really wished that she had caught the vision like Michael, who had even changed his major from computer science to business management, like his dad.

Chapter 43

It was decided that the twins would go live with their father while they went to college. Michelle wasn't too excited about going, but I tried hard to convince her that it was best so that she wouldn't have to struggle so hard while working different jobs like she had seen me do for so long. Michael was ready to go but had concerns about leaving me. The evening before the twins were to go back to their father, when no one else was around, Michael came into the kitchen and looked me right in the eyes.

"Ma?"

"Huh?"

"Are you going to be okay?"

"Yeah, I'll be okay. I don't want you worrying about me. All I want you to do is go down there and get a good education so that you can get a good job and be suc—" Usually I could turn a conversation around with Michael pretty easily but he didn't let me get away with it this time.

"Ma?"

"What?"

"I'm worried about you, Ma. I mean, I don't want Terrell to hurt you. I mean, you know, like *physically* hurt you. You got to promise me that you won't let him do that to you, Ma."

It was a promise that I knew I had to make if I really didn't want the twins to worry about me.

"I won't, I promise." Michael looked at me for a few seconds longer as if he was trying to decide whether he could believe me or not. Then he turned and walked away.

The twins had to leave the day after graduation, because James came to see them graduate and didn't want to make another trip back to get them only a month and a half later, when they were scheduled to start college.

I didn't feel too good on the day they graduated and couldn't decide if what I was feeling was real or just all in my mind because the twins were leaving. It seemed so final when they left, because they didn't just take a lot of clothes, CDs, and other things like children normally take with them to college. James actually rented a U-Haul so that they could take their furniture with them. I really couldn't stand it, but I knew the time had to come sooner or later and I didn't want them to see me crack.

Right before they left, I pulled them together to talk to them one last time. I wanted to say something powerful enough to really stick, but at the same time, I had to make it fast, because James was waiting in the U-Haul with the motor running. I was trying real hard to stretch the time as far as I could, but I could stretch it no further; it was time for them to go. I put my arms around their shoulders.

"I just want to let you guys know that up until this point, you really have made me super proud of you, because, first of all, you went through twelve long years of school and I didn't have to come one day during the whole twelve behind either of ya'll cutting up."

Michelle looked at Michael and smiled; then they both started laughing.

"What?" I asked, with a frown and smile on my face at the same time, determined to let nothing spoil the moment. Michelle was the one bold enough to tell it.

"Well, a few times we *did* get in trouble but we negotiated our way out of it, because we *knew* if you came to that school . . ." We all started laughing.

"Anyway, I want you guys to know that I love you from the bottom of my heart, and please don't go down there and get in no trouble. Don't do like me and get sidetracked. Put your education first. This way, if you make a mistake in life, you can pay for it much easier. And don't worry about me—I'll be okay. Just concentrate on what you're there for, and just like you made me proud of you as children, make me proud of you as adults, ya'll hear me?"

They promised that they would and then they got in James's car, Michael in the driver's seat and Michelle on the passenger side. James pulled off behind them in the U-Haul.

I stood in the same spot and didn't take my eyes off the car and truck until they were completely out of sight. A little earlier, I'd looked over at the apartments that were close to our house and had seen a group of guys drinking beer. After I couldn't see James and the twins anymore, I looked over there again, and although the group was still there, I could see no one except Terrell. He was looking right back at me. Slowly I went into the house. . . .

Chapter 44

The house seemed totally different with the twins not there anymore. To make matters worse, Terrell turned Michael's room into a weight-lifting room and Michelle's room into Terra's room. Even though Terra had previously shared the room with Michelle anyway, it looked more like a little girl's room when Michelle left. Terrell continued to show off every now and then, but he really seemed to be trying to do better and I remained hopeful.

Although I had my hands full between getting Terra prepared for school and getting the school prepared for Terra, I was still depressed when I saw the school bus come to pick up the high school kids that September.

The twins kept in continual contact with me on the phone. Michael was okay, but Michelle was miserable. I think their personalities had a lot to do with it, because Michael immediately got a job and started making friends. Michelle, on the other hand, was still funny about whom she chose to be bothered with, and even more than that, she was in a whole new state. She had no problem letting me know how much she hated it, and it really bothered me, because I knew that regardless of how unhappy she was, it was the best thing for her. Still, she was my child and I hated to see her so unhappy.

On top of everything else, James couldn't understand why the twins weren't responding to him about certain things the way he felt they should've, and lots of times they argued with him. I wanted so bad to tell him that it was because he hadn't been around when they had needed him the most, and they were all grown up now, so whatever he felt he was doing for them, they more than likely could do for themselves, and didn't he know that the way he thought he was hiding from me all those years would come back on him in one way or another? I wanted to fuss him out so many times, but I didn't, because the twins asked me not to and I didn't want to make their living conditions any harder than they already were.

Before I knew it, it was Christmas and the twins were back home for the holiday. I was hoping that Terrell wouldn't show off too bad so that the twins would believe that I was okay while they were gone. He seemed to do okay, much to my surprise, but as soon as they left, he really poured it on.

I had to go to work the night they left and he was supposed to be there to watch Terra. As usual, he was over at the apartments that were near our house drinking, getting high, and God knows what else. I was already in trouble for being late to work all the time, so I went to find him and tell him to hurry up. Right when I was headed toward the apartments, I saw him walking away from them. I thought he was coming home, but instead, he turned the other way toward the store. I called out to him, but he kept walking as though he never heard me. I went in the house and called my boss and told him that I would be late *again.* When I went back out to try to find Terrell, he was standing in front of the apartments with another guy. I told him to come on home because I had to go to work. He said that he wasn't ready to come right then. We started arguing and I started to cry, which embarrassed him, so he came in but we continued to argue.

"I don't see why I got to stay in the house. I'll be right back. She'll be all right by herself."

"Terrell, you not going back out."

"You don't tell me what to do, woman. . . ."

Before I knew it, we got into a shoving match, and I called the police. After we both told the police officer our stories, he turned to Terrell.

"Is this your baby?"

"Yeah, that's my seed," Terrell answered the policeman, sounding as dumb as he possibly could.

"That's your what?" The policeman had a frown of confusion on his face.

"My seed," Terrell repeated. I was so embarrassed.

"Then why wouldn't you want to stay home to watch your own baby so that your wife can go to work?"

"I *am* at home. I'm just standing outside. I can see my house from where I'ma be standing."

"Those guys that hang out there all either deal or use drugs. You have a family and don't need to be out there," the policeman said as he looked at Terrell.

"That's what I keep trying to tell—" The policeman held his hand up to signal me to be quiet but never took his eyes off of Terrell. He probably was trying to get Terrell to tell on himself or the other guys. After continuing to try to reason with Terrell, he got tired of arguing with him.

"Give me your cell phone number and go ahead to work," the policeman said to me.

"But, Mr. Policeman, I don't want to get in no trouble for our baby being by herself if he leave this house again," I said.

"Don't worry about it, you're not going to get in any trouble. Just go ahead and do like I said." Then he turned to Terrell.

"Sir, I'm going to be patrolling this area, and I *don't* want to see you back outside. If I do see you, I'll call your wife to come back home, and then you will be arrested and put in jail. Do you understand?" Terrell didn't answer him, just went to the couch and sat down. I left for work, but something kept telling me to go back home.

When I walked back into my house, I almost passed out. It was destroyed again and Terrell was sitting there drinking. Not just beer this time, which is the only thing I'd seen him drink in the past, but liquor straight from one of those flat, dark brown bottles. I didn't say anything at first, just started cleaning up the mess. I was really hurt, but he was either too drunk to notice or didn't care, because when I didn't respond like he thought I would, he started saying things to me and calling me names that I couldn't believe. I fought to hold back the tears while I finally starting fussing back at him.

"You know you really are one ignorant, dumb black man! Don't get mad at *me* because you supposed to be a man and the police had you scared to leave your own house!" I yelled.

After we finished arguing and he saw that I wasn't going back to work, he figured that he didn't have to stay home anymore, but instead of just leaving, he picked up the phone and called a woman to come get him—right in front of my face. I felt something inside me snap. I started cussing him out like never before. Then I said something to him that I automatically knew was a mistake as soon as I said it.

"Just go ahead and go over your woman's house so that I can call *my* man to come over here and . . ." I never got to finish the sentence. Terrell jumped off the couch, grabbed me around the throat, and started dragging me. He didn't stop dragging me until my back was against the wall and I was begging him to let me go. As soon as he let me go, I ran to the phone and called 911.

While we waited for the police to come, he continued to argue with me.

"I knew all along you had somebody else!" Then he went and got a stick. I crouched down in the corner begging him not to hit me. I couldn't believe what was happening to me and wondered what was taking the police so long and what kind of shape I would be in when they finally got there.

Soon the police arrived, and after listening to our stories, they handcuffed Terrell to take him to jail. As soon as the police car pulled off, the woman Terrell had called to come get him pulled up. I made eye contact with the woman, then slowly closed the door and finished cleaning up the mess. The whole time I was cleaning up I was thinking about how Terrell could have the nerve to go off on me like that after I had only *insinuated* that I had someone else after he had cheated on me so many times without even *trying* to hide it. The part that hurt me the most was that of *all* the men I'd had relationships with, Terrell was the only man I'd ever been faithful to the whole time, regardless of all the heartache he had put me through. The *only* man. There were so many times when I had the opportunity to cheat as well as times when I should have, but I didn't. I thought about the very first time I saw him and when he gave his number to my coworker to give to me. I thought about the kind of life we could've had together had it not been for him choosing the drugs and drinking over me. I thought about the twins being almost grown when I'd decided to have another baby just for him. Oh, well, it didn't matter anymore, because then I thought about my promise to Michael and knew what I had to do. Not just for Michael, but more importantly for myself . . .

I was glad that Terra didn't hear me crying as I thought of my last fight with Terrell. I went into the bathroom to wash my face, because it was so drenched from tears that I knew my mere hands wouldn't do the job this time.

Chapter 45

So here I am, blessed with a nice two-bedroom apartment that I got with Gloria's help. The morning I moved, Terrell knew nothing about my plans. He saw me packing a few days earlier, but he didn't believe that I was really moving, because I had threatened to do it so many times before. When the day finally came, I called Gloria to see if she could help. She told me to just call her back when I was ready. As soon as Terrell's work truck turned the corner, I called her.

"I'm ready."

"I'm on my way."

She, her oldest son, her niece, her nephew, and her brother-in-law were soon there. Everything I couldn't take with me, I either sold in the front yard at the same time I was moving or gave away. The apartment that I was moving into was on the second floor and the kids were so tired that they just threw everything in the front room. I was so happy to have their help that I dared not complain.

"I feel like I should be giving them *something*," I

kept repeating to Gloria in a low voice so that the kids couldn't hear me.

"Girl, please. They better not even *think* of asking for nothing," Gloria answered, without even looking back at me. By the time Terrell got home from work that day, I was gone. . . .

That night, I was so tired I could hardly move. Mom told me not to worry about coming to get Terra, because she knew how tired I was and that I still had so much more to do. I went to a nearby Hardee's and got a half gallon of tea. I finally found my couch and cleared off just enough space to sit down. Even though my back was hurting like never before, my legs were numb, and I had a terrible headache, I felt like a weight had been lifted off my shoulders. I couldn't remember falling asleep on the couch, but when I woke I felt better. Then I took a look around me and figured I might as well get started, but I knew I had something to do first. I knew that I needed to spend my very first morning in my new apartment in prayer. . . .

I was always taught that when you pray, you are supposed to thank God for all He's already blessed you with before you ask for something else, and I truly had some things to ask for.

I first thanked God for keeping me in my right mind while I was with Terrell and letting me finally get strength and courage enough to leave him. Then I thanked Him for my family: Mom, Liz, Clarita, and Jr. Then I thanked Him for my children: Michael, Michelle, and Terra. Then I thanked Him for my friends who stuck by me all through the years, especially Gloria, because she had stood by me through three life-changing things that I know I would never have been able to go through alone. The first was going back to college to finish my education. The second was finding out about Terra's disability. The third was physically leaving Terrell. . . .

Finally, I felt like I could start asking Him for the things that I needed, and the most important thing I knew that I needed was His forgiveness. I was also taught that God forgives all except self-murder and blasphemy of the Holy Ghost. It was apparent that I hadn't murdered myself, although, to be completely honest, there were times when I'd seriously considered it. Then I tried to remember if I had ever blasphemed the Holy Ghost. Again, I thought about the red blouse and my confrontation with God when I was five or six years old in Ohio. All of a sudden I realized that I had never really repented for cussing God out. I may not have known better when I was at that young age, but I certainly knew better now. I had finally come to realize that the reason I felt God was holding this act against me as well as punishing me for it was that I'd never really repented for it. Everything else that I had to ask for I put on hold. I knew that this was much more important. Only after I prayed for forgiveness did I realize that He had already forgiven me but that I had not forgiven myself. Only after I prayed for forgiveness did I not feel like I was being punished anymore for cussing God out when I was a child in the little dim room upstairs at 254 N. Vine Avenue in Cleveland, Ohio. . . .

* * *

Standing in the bathroom, I took a good look at myself and the tears that flowed down my face from reliving the plethora of memories.

Lord, have mercy, girl, will you get yourself together? Will you ever stop crying? Take a minute to count your blessings. You're back in college full-time and doing pretty well for someone who's also a single parent and working a full-time job. [On my first semester back, I made all Bs and one C—a 2.87 grade point average.] *The twins are in college and living with their father, a professor. How can they fail? Most importantly, you can finally rest assured that Terrell won't wake you up in the middle of the night by doing something stupid trying to get to his drugs or other women.*

Things really were finally looking up.

Gloria had long said good-bye, and the apartment looked great. I went to the living room, plopped down on the couch beside my daughter, and wrapped my arms around her.

"I love you so much, Terra."

She looked up at me and smiled.

"I love you too, Ma."

And forgive us our debts, as we forgive our debtors.
Matthew 6:12 KJV

A Note from the Author

Although I was advised not to let anyone read this book until after it was published, I still let my very best friend read it, because I was anxious to know what someone else thought and I was confident that she would be totally honest with me. Right after she read the very last sentence, she gave me a call. It was all of 2:00 in the morning, but I didn't mind, because I knew exactly why she was calling. This was our conversation:

"Hey, girl."

"Don't tell me that you finished it that quick."

"I did."

"And?"

She let out a deep breath and I got nervous, because I immediately jumped to the conclusion that she was trying not to hurt my feelings.

"Ivy, I think it was awesome. You've been through a lot, girl."

Somehow what she said didn't seem like enough for me.

"Well, let me ask you something. If you didn't know me and you just happened to pick the book up, would it have held your interest in the same way, or did you just keep reading it because you know me?"

"It would've held my interest in the same way."

"Please be honest. . . ."

"Why don't you believe me?"

"Because you sound half dead."

"You know what time it is? I *am* half dead. But I still didn't stop reading until I was finished so that should tell you something, right?"

"I guess so. . . ."

"Lord, girl. I see you ain't gonna let me rest until I tell you everything I'm thinking, so here goes."

"Yeah?"

"It made me feel like I was watching a movie. You know that you always were such a vivid writer. But, Ivy, can I ask you something?"

"Anything."

"There are so many other things that you could've written about, so why did you write about yourself? I mean, why would you want to put all your business out for the whole world to read like that?"

"Well, first of all, it's not quite all of my business. Some things that I've been through, I'll *never* tell. Never. But recently, I had a conversation with my pastor about periods of time that were missing from the Bible, like the period when there were dinosaurs, or the period when Adam and Eve had children before they had Cain and Abel, and he told me that these periods of time weren't mentioned because they had no real significance in God's plan of salvation to man. So to answer your question, I only wrote about things that had some sort of significance in my life. About things that have helped me in some way or another become the person that I am today. You know that I've never been a very private person anyway, because I believe that everything happens for a reason. Everything. So the way I figure is if these things have helped me, then maybe, just maybe, they'll help somebody else."

"How?"

"Well, for one thing, it'll help people understand that regardless of what they went through in life, even as a child, it had a purpose. It'll let single parents and parents of special-needs children, who are really struggling, know that they are not alone. It'll let women who are in abusive relationships see themselves as the outsider looking in and hopefully do something about their situation. It'll let people know that it is never too late to give up on their dreams. It'll make people not take their family and close friends for granted. . . . Need I go on?"

"Well, yeah, but not just for me. Put it in the sequel."